ADVENTURES IN DECEPTION

PART-II

DIAMOND KEY

ISBN: Number
Paperback: 978-1-966968-07-8
Hard Cover: 978-1-966968-56-6
eBook: 978-1-966968-57-3

Published by:

PUBLISHERS
www.owlpublishers.com

360 S Market St, San Jose, CA 95113,
United States.

Printed in the United States of America

About the Author

My name is Lakesha Dorsey Maldonado but my close friends and family call me KeyKey. I'm a mother of three grown kids and grandmother of two. I grew up in Howard County in a large loving family. I have always loved meeting new people. I was told at an early age that I've had a very active imagination. So what better way to share my wild imagination was to start writing. I started writing little short stories as a young girl. I expressed myself by creating stories or whatever came to mind along with writing poetry. My dream is to open a shop or two to sell my books, my customized bracelets along with creating my own clothing line called Simply Key or Simply Diamond? Be my own Boss. My Mom always told me I could do or be anything I wanted to be. And I shall full fill that Destiny.

Table of Content

Introduction

Jayla is what you call your normal typical teenage girl who is living with her single parent dad named Aiden who is a cop in the rural suburbs of Atlanta. Jayla is excited because, she is looking forward to graduating out of high school to start her life with her boyfriend named Shane so she thought? Jayla's world is crushed after she finds out that her boyfriend Shane is moving to another city after graduation because, Shane's dad was offered a new job in a different city three hours away? Jayla's dad comes home one morning and, starts packing and tells her to do the same quickly without an explanation? Jayla quickly does as she is told and jumps into the vehicle as Aiden tells Jayla and her best friend Dayonna are going on a vacation across country. Jayla tries to call Shane put gets a shock when she overhears a girl in the background telling him to hurry off the phone that leaves Jayla heartbroken thinking that the love of her life has found another woman? While Jayla and Dayonna are taking in the sights of the town, Jayla discovers they are being followed by a strange acting man but, what's even stranger it looks like the same man from her dreams which have been coming quite frequently today for some reason. Soon Jayla is having a difficult time after she discovers a family secret only to be followed by other family secrets of her family and past? But Jayla is not the only one who is told about some secrets from the past? Aiden is also hit with a few secrets that was kept from him as well from his past? As other secrets unfold within the family, Jayla is faced with a reality she didn't see or think of happening to her? Jayla is processing the secrets only to be bombarded with a secret of all secrets, Aiden is also told about this secret but will this secret be too big for Jayla to get over? Will this one secret that was told be the cause of Jayla's biggest heart break?

Just because, you are bonded with someone for keeping their secret doesn't mean that the secret won't find a way to come out but at the wrong time and, have you and the others involved second questing about everyone you know and everything you know? Adventures in Deception is another book by Diamond Key that will have you yelling at the book one minute, blushing in certain parts and laughing out loud in other parts.

Reader's Note for Transition to Part Two

Thank you for joining Jayla on the first part of her journey, filled with love, family, and self-discovery. As her story continues, secrets unravel, danger emerges, and Jayla must navigate a world far more complex than she ever imagined. Turn the page to embark on the second part of her adventure and uncover the truth behind Shane's deception and its ties to her family's hidden past.

Chapter 1:
Why is my ex Shane on my Dad's radar?

So the next day, we had a Mother and Daughter Spa Day. My Mom and I arrived at the spa and were greeted by the nicest saleslady named Sara. She first took us to the back and offered Mom some wine to relax. Mom told her to get me one. This is our secret, my Mom replied, raising her glass. I told her this secret is safe with me and raised my glass.

I told my mom how I felt about Alex. I really talked to her about what I was thinking about doing. It's so nice to talk to you, Mom, about anything, including sex? I said that because talking to Uncle Aiden was like a brick wall. Besides, I would always be his little Princess. The thought of me having sex freaked him out.

While Jayla and Katiana were in the spa, talking and enjoying their spa treatment. Shane was lurking in the spa, trying to see what Jayla was doing.

After my talk with my mom, she told me we would take a trip to the family doctor without my dad knowing, of course.

Mommy, this is not my first time, I said.

I assumed it wasn't, Mommy replied. I just want you to make sure you are healthy and free from any STDs. That's what moms do, get used to it she replied. We make sure everyone is well and safe at all times.

When we got back home, Daddy called me into his office to talk. I started snooping by his desk and noticed a picture of my ex-boyfriend, Shane.

Now, why does Daddy have a picture of my ex-boyfriend Shane? Why does it say Arturo, not Shane, gave me even more reasons to think?

Before I walked into the back part of his office, I stopped. I heard Daddy on the phone talking to someone about how he hated this guy named Arturo and hoped he or Aiden would never run into him.

So when Dad opened up his back door, he said, Sorry, Blue Jay, important phone call. I don't want to scare you, but something has come up. I want to talk to you about what your mom and I discussed earlier.

There is a guy named Arturo who used to work for me and your uncle Aiden. He used to be Head of Security? Like Mr. Stan, I said, interrupting? Daddy said, long story short, he was caught sending information to our enemy. And then he badly hurt one of my other guys who was working for the family?

Aiden warned me about him, but I didn't listen to him until it was too late. Daddy replied, looking mad. He hurt one of my guards, Daniel, badly? So he couldn't work for us anymore. And I still take care of him and his family to this day. He is still on my payroll, like nothing ever happened. We treat him as a retired employee, so he and his family are taken care of for life.

When I finally fired Arturo, he looked at me and Aiden and told us he would make us sorry he was ever fired. On his way out, he told Aiden to watch his back because when he decides to come, we won't know what hit him.

After what happened to Daniel, Aiden became ready to take revenge on him sooner or later.

Daddy then showed me this recent picture of Arturo, seen in or around town? In case I saw him in town, or if I try to come to the house? He looks like this, Daddy said, then walked back to his chair. He showed me a picture of Shane, my ex-boyfriend. What the hell runs through my mind?

I pretended not to know him at first, but then I teared up.

This is Arturo, the guy that you and Uncle Aiden fired years ago, I replied, trying to take all the conversation in.

Yes, he is a very dangerous and abusive man with a military background. Daddy then said he has ways to be around while hiding in

2

plain sight. So if you see him or think you saw him. Please tell me or your uncle Aiden, all right, Blue Jay?

Chapter 2:
Thank You for Choosing Me

The next day, I got a phone call from Dayonna. They won't be coming along with us on Christmas vacation? They're staying with Ms. Sharon so she won't be alone during the holidays. They won't be able to join us for Christmas in Disney World, so we're heading to another place during New Year's. It's a surprise, I told Dayonna.

It's a surprise where you're spending your New Year's Eve, Dayonna replied?

Yes, and I pray it's near a beach and a mall so we can do some after-Christmas shopping for Aunt Kelani's baby, Jayla says.

Now that Alex works with Daddy as the errand boy, delivering papers, we spend more time together. My Dad has a business that deals with traveling for businesses and properties. Alex helps people plan their trips out of state or within the state. At least Alex doesn't have to worry about staying away long or putting in time for leave, I think, laughing.

I would sometimes meet Alex at work while checking in on Daddy and Uncle Aiden. Alex and I would eat on the rooftop. There's a company restaurant with an amazing view, which is why we eat up there.

Uncle Aiden left a message on Dad's email stating he hoped to be back at the house before they left for Disney. And that he had some new information about Arturo?

Grandma Ida and Grandpa Vince told Mommy that they would arrive on Thursday, before we leave. They were doing last-minute preparations for the trip. Daddy always told Mommy that if their parents got too old to be alone, he would have them stay with them on the ground in another part of the house. So they would still have their privacy. Alex is upset that Kirk won't be with them on Christmas, but maybe they could join us for New Year's? Daddy said if they could make it, he would send the plane to go get them.

Dad's guard friend was home and healing nicely. Looking forward to getting back to work with the family?

Kelani called, saying she was getting a baby bump. Zander was getting excited about her baby bump growing. She said she needed more clothes because she was fluctuating between gaining and losing weight. Her old ones were starting to get tight, and then they would feel loose. So her doctor told her to keep an eye on that?

Mom and Aunt Kelani were talking about finding some family stuff to do. Some of the stuff she wanted to do, they couldn't because of her surprise pregnancy. And Zander doesn't want to jeopardize that.

Aiden will be here sometime tonight. Katiana smiles after deleting his message. Can't wait to see him, she thought. She had to admit she had missed him. And he will always be her heart.

Giovanni called Aiden on the plane and told him they would talk after his meeting with the guys. Giovanni got home from his meeting with some of the other Mafia top men. Mommy and I ate dinner alone that day.

Mommy told me she hated it when Daddy met with other people from the Mafia. Even though Dad was not alone, she still worried about him. But she knew he was in good hands, always with Henry. Besides, Aiden was now back; he always had his back. Stan is always close by as well, always ready in case something pops off?

I excuse myself to look through my closet for some clothes to take on the trip. Or perhaps see if she needed to go shopping for some new clothes to pack? Besides, I wanted to talk to Alex and see if he wanted to hang out for a bit. It was only six, but it seemed way later than that.

When I hung up with Alex, I heard my mom talking to someone, but who? As I come around the corner to tell mom something? See her talking to Uncle Aiden? I overheard him tell my mom?

You will always be my Kit Kat, Uncle Aiden replied to her as he grabbed her hand.

Mommy went to walk away as Uncle Aiden pulled her to him, and they shared a passionate kiss.

Do you think it's easy seeing you with my brother Giovanni, Aiden asked my mom?

But instead of smacking my uncle, my mom kissed him passionately back?

I crept back up the stairs, holding my mouth in disbelief. What the hell I just walked in on, I say to myself. Mommy was kissing my uncle Aiden? Is my mom cheating on my dad with my uncle?

I'm a Daddy's little girl, but I love my uncle as well. So I try to shake off the image of seeing my mom and Uncle Aiden kissing. I mean, Mommy was kissing him like she kissed my daddy? I caught them a couple of times.

Mommy knocked on the door as I was having a private conversation with myself inside my head. Can I come in, Blue Jay she asked.

Mommy begins talking to me, and I don't know how to act towards her after what I witnessed. Your uncle Aiden is here, maybe you should go say hi, she says. Maybe later, Mommy, he might be tired from his flight?

Then mommy says something, not sure what, and I just snap at her.

Mommy looked at me with a shocked look on her face. What's the problem with you, Blue Jay?

Nothing, Mommy just wanted to tell you I was going out with Alex for a few? We're going to the park to hear some music.

Blue Jay, something is bothering you as she picks up my face? Tell me, baby girl, what has you upset?

Really, Mommy, you act like you didn't do anything wrong, I replied. What are you talking about, Blue Jay? Why were you and my uncle Aiden kissing in the living room a few minutes ago? I was on my way to tell you that Alex and I were going out for a few hours this evening. When I heard you talking to someone as I came around the corner to see. I'm looking at you and my uncle Aiden sharing a passionate kiss?

Mommy looked at me, shocked that they got caught. Jayla, let me explain, reaching for my hand? I pull away, please, she says calmly, grabbing my hand.

Mommy, I don't want to be the reason why Daddy and Uncle Aiden don't talk anymore.

Jayla, there's something about me and your uncle Aiden that you don't know? We were close friends, well more than friends, she said, then swallowed hard. We were together for five years, engaged to get married.

One night, I was on my way to tell Aiden I was late and needed to get checked out. I saw Aiden messing around with another girl through his open blinds. So, I ran to the garden and started crying, my mom says.

Giovanni saw me and asked me what was wrong. We got something to eat and then went back to the house. That night, I slept with Giovanni to try to get over Aiden. Did it work? I asked my Mommy. No answer?

A few months later, we found out I was pregnant with you. I never checked the piece of paper to see if I was pregnant the night I ran into the garden where Giovanni saw me. But by the time I found out I was pregnant with you? Giovanni and I had fallen in love, Mommy replied, tearing up.

Aiden had clearly moved on with someone out of state, so I assumed. Giovanni never told your uncle Aiden what happened between us, and he stayed with me to give you a family.

Aiden had a fight with Giovanni about someone or something, not sure, and then he just left. Then you already know about why, well, somewhat why he took you for your safety? It was hard to find you for several years. We couldn't get any information about Aiden, as if he had vanished.

Today, seeing Aiden brought back some feelings, and we got carried away. That young hurt girl will always love her first one?

I will always love your uncle Aiden, mommy replies, but I love your daddy. I would not do anything to hurt him. Some things are best not said and kept in the past, Mom said, wiping her eyes.

Mommy, is Dad really my dad or?

I'm sorry, Mommy. I didn't mean to make you cry, I told her, hugging her.

That was my goodbye kiss to your uncle Aiden? Do I ever wonder how my life would have been with him? Of course I do, Blue Jay, but?

Still half crying, but I love the life my husband, your father, has given us.

Are we fine, Blue Jay, my Mom asked me in tears?

Yes, we are fine, Mommy, and promise not to bring it up again.

Thank you for telling me the truth, Mommy? I know it wasn't easy.

Mommy says, Jayla, one day we will talk about my past?

Another time, I promised Jayla, then she left, wiping her eyes as she did. Now I feel bad for my Mom, she's upset. A few hours later, Giovanni comes walking into the front door.

Kat, honey, I'm back, and I kiss her on the forehead. Where is Blue Jay, Giovanni asked Katiana.

She's at the park with Alex, will be back in a few. Are you hungry,

8

Giovanni, Katiana asked?

Yeah, he says. I'll tell Ms. Gracie to warm up a plate for you, Katiana says.

Hey Vanni, can I tell you something? Trying not to get emotional, Katiana asked him.

Yeah, Katiana, you can ask me anything, Giovanni replied, holding her.

Have I ever told you that I appreciate the life you have given me, Giovanni, Katiana says.

It was my pleasure to take care of you and our daughter, Giovanni answered, holding her. When I saw you crying in the garden years ago, you were so distraught. And that's when I decided to make you mine, showing you there was another option.

And that night when we made love, Katiana? I knew that I had made the best decision.

Aiden had been listening to the whole conversation and started reliving that night when he and Katiana had broken up.

Damn, Katiana got with my older brother Giovanni because of me? Aiden tells himself, I drove my lover into the arms of another man? My older brother had to be the other man. Aiden shook his head in disgust. Kit Kat, I will always love you, Aiden whispered to himself. I never stopped loving you, Kit Kat, but clearly you don't feel the same way, or do you?

Aiden goes back into his room and starts looking at some old pictures of him and Katiana.

Chapter 3:
Someone's Past is beginning to Surface?

Aiden begins to share with Giovanni and Stan what the police in North Carolina discovered the next morning. They had found the body of a young woman along with an older couple that is believed to be her parents, in the living room of a home.

The men working with Aiden showed him pictures. Aiden saw the pictures and found out later that it was Shane's ex-girlfriend, Allissa. Whom had he left to be with Jayla? She was the one who answered Shane's phone, which upset Jayla. Aiden had heard Jayla and Dayonna talking in the back, pretending not to listen. And the older couple he knew was Andrew and Carmen Fredrickson? He later found out that he had posed as Shane's parents, but really the parents of Allisa? They had been shot execution-style.

He killed them because he was being blackmailed, and they threatened to tell on him, Aiden explains to Giovanni and Stan. Allissa was three months pregnant and stabbed in her stomach over thirty-two times.

Aiden is even more disgusted by Shane/Arturo, knowing those people were in his home. Aiden, you have to forgive yourself, Aiden repeats to himself. It's not your fault you didn't know what that psycho was capable of?

Shane had been following me around town for weeks. Getting more unhinged and ready to explode. Shane left a message for me to come see him alone. He wants us to remain friends? I deleted all his messages and then blocked that number as well.

Shane then left a nasty message when he saw me in town kissing Alex, which made him madder. Seeing me with someone other than him?

We stopped by the house before heading to Alex's house to get something I wanted to borrow. That's when Daddy and Uncle Aiden shared with me what they found out about Arturo's ex-girlfriend, Allissa, and her parents.

Allissa was found murdered and was pregnant, stabbed in her stomach over thirty-two times. Along with her parents, Andrew and Carmen, Aiden explained.

I broke down, couldn't keep my secret from Daddy anymore. I'm sorry, Daddy, but that is my ex-boyfriend, Shane. How? Why didn't you say something? I didn't know who he was, Aiden replied. He's very good at changing his appearance, Giovanni says.

I didn't know, Princess. My job is to keep you safe, and I feel like I failed, Aiden replied. He's very good at disguises, Giovanni said.

Aiden, you taught him well, Giovanni says, looking worried for Aiden.

A bit too damn well, Aiden says, throwing his glass on the floor, which made me jump.

It disgusted me that he killed Allissa, and it was probably their unborn child she was carrying. I looked at the pictures and, sadly, he killed her parents like that as well. He's one sick bastard, I told Uncle Aiden, giving him a hug.

Blue Jay, it's not your fault or my fault? I need to run your phone for some clues, Uncle Aiden told me.

Go ahead, and then you can change the number in case he tries to contact me? I need to clear my head and start crying. This is a lot to take in, I tell myself, trying to get those images out of my head.

I told Alex, who was waiting for me on the porch. That something came up, and I needed time to be by myself? I just had to get those images of what Shane did to those people and how my dad looked. As I told him that we had dated this man for five years?

Knock, knock, Jayla, can Mommy please come in?

Yeah, Ma sure as I wipe my tears. Stop beating yourself up, honey?

11

You had no clue who he was? He even fooled your uncle Aiden?

That's not as easy as you think my mom replied. Aiden is very good at his job. I have to tell you exactly what your uncle does at another time, she replied.

Mommy, I had sex with this man, and to hear those things he did, along with his past, makes me feel so dirty.

Shane, Arturo, whatever his name is? I used to let him touch me, kiss me? Oh God, Mommy, what if he wanted to do that to me, I said.

Jayla, you have to try not to think about that. Your uncle and dad will find him, Mommy says. Pray on it, and it will give you some inner peace. We all have done something in life that we wish we could go back and change.

Daddy must hate me after what I told him. I told my Mom? Before my Mom could answer a knock comes on my door?

Knock, knock, Princess may we come in Daddy asked?

We could never hate you, and it's not your fault. That's what I keep on telling your uncle Aiden, who is beating himself up. Just like you, and it's not either one of your faults, Arturo is good at what he does. Your new phone will be here in the morning with all your contacts already programmed, Uncle Aiden says, standing behind Giovanni.

Daddy loves you so much, Mommy says. Jayla, we will always love you, Uncle Aiden replies.

Stan and Uncle Aiden found some things that could possibly help locate Shane or Arturo. Whatever his real name is? Get some rest, Blue Jay; you have had an emotional day. We all have patted Aiden to try and comfort his brother, who was still having a hard time forgiving his self.

Alex called while you were talking to your mom, Uncle Aiden told me. What did he say, Uncle Aiden, I asked.

He said that he loves you and will be here for breakfast.

Alex is a good man, and my Dad and uncle Aiden replied as my Mom nodded her head in agreement with them. And you get a pass, my uncle Aiden replied.

Thank you, Uncle Aiden, you mean a lot to me, I told him.

Night, Blue Jay, you get some rest, my parents say as they leave my room. Mommy glanced at Uncle Aiden, and half smiled in his direction.

Never realized how much you look like your auntie Dalilah, uncle Aiden says, tearing up. Daddy turned around and smiled and agreed.

I hugged my uncle Aiden because I loved him. Nite, and you get some sleep as well. Uncle Aiden says, I have to tell you about your auntie at another time. I lay down in my bed as things still ran through my mind. Who really was this Shane or Arturo guy? And why did he get involved with me? Why did he come into my life? I wonder what my aunt Dalilah was like? Does my uncle Aiden still think about my Mommy? I need to stop thinking about this shit? Why did he kill Allissa and her family? Am I next? Will he try to kill me, too? God, please take those images from my mind? Shane, you killed her and your unborn baby? You are a sick bastard, and I hope we never meet again. I can't help yawning; I can't keep my eyes open any longer. Mommy eased my door open and told my daddy that I had finally dozed off, and then they went to bed. They didn't go to sleep because they were worried about me? That night I dreamed about Alex and me. I dreamed we were getting married, and everyone was so happy for us. But then all of a sudden Shane showed up and tried to get me, and I jumped up. I held my bear Alex won for me. I could still smell his cologne, so I hugged it tight and soon dozed off once again.

Chapter 4:
Holiday Blessings in Abundance?

I had woken up earlier that next morning. Hadn't gotten much sleep, and my mind was racing all night. I kept thinking about what my father told her about Shane or Arturo.

It was hard because we were once in a relationship. And not once did this man ever slip up, I thought? This man, whom I loved once upon a time. Killed his ex-girlfriend, their unborn child, and her parents? And left them in the house to rot, I thought?

The Shane, aka Arturo, I knew was always kind, sometimes a jerk. But he was never like that towards me, as he was described last night?

Now I'm wondering if he'll come after her because I didn't return his calls or meet him as he wanted. As I think about it, I'm getting emotional.

But I know that Daddy and my uncle Aiden, along with his men, will make sure I'm always safe. But then I remembered the nasty voicemail he left, which I deleted. Now he knows about Alex and me? Will he try to do something to him if he can't get to me, runs through my mind?

As we sit down to eat breakfast. We hear some sort of commotion outside. Aiden gets up and tells Giovanni he will see what's going on outside. And for them to continue to get ready to eat and report back? Mr. Stan followed my uncle Aiden as we looked. After breakfast, they meet in Giovanni's office. What is it, Aiden, Giovanni asked his brother.

The guardsmen found a dead fox and a message along with it. Aiden says to Giovanni in his ear? The message read, Death is coming here, so hug your loved ones, keep them near?

Aiden hits the wall with his fist. Arturo has been on these grounds. Arturo has been saying that bastard is going to pay when I find him, Aiden says, not noticing his fist.

Aiden calls Henry and tells him what he found. Henry, we need you at the house like yesterday, Aiden tells him. Making sure our family is safe is now our main priority, Giovanni tells Aiden as he nods.

Aiden tells the guards, and they start walking around the house again. Sorry, we couldn't continue breakfast with you all this morning, something came up, "Giovanni says.

"What's wrong, Giovanni? Now I'm really worried, Katiana says.

A wild animal was in the middle of the driveway, and they were trying to scare it. Giovanni replied quickly, trying to convince Katiana.

Mommy, Daddy, we are going to Black Rock Hot Springs for the day to relax. We are going to sit in one of the hot springs, I said. Sounds like fun, my dad and uncle say.

You two have fun and make sure you keep in touch, my dad said in a concerned voice.

We began to leave and noticed a car following us a short distance. But we were used to that, so it seemed normal.

Giovanni, you need to be honest with Katiana, Aiden replied.

What's going on, Giovanni, Katiana asked him.

Aiden, please tell me the truth, Katiana asked, looking concerned.

We think Arturo has been here because we found a dead animal with a note attached to it, Aiden said. Katiana glanced at Giovanni, giving him that pissed look.

Where did you find the note and what did it say, Katiana asked Aiden.

It had to be someplace to get you that pissed off and hit this wall? Yeah, you didn't think I heard that and noticed his fist is now swelling?

Guards found it near Jayla's window and fingerprints on the glass door to her room. Giovanni replied, looking at Katiana's face.

That sick bastard was watching my Blue Jay as she slept, Katiana says, getting enraged.

I will kill that mother fucker myself and not break a nail?

Kit Kat, calm down, we have got some things in place, Aiden says. Our family's safety is our main priority.

We will make sure Arturo will not hurt anyone in this house or family, Giovanni says.

Stan is installing additional security measures on the grounds, including silent motion sensors, which Aiden designed, according to Giovanni, who informs Katiana. Arturo has a Momma bear to worry about now? And that's way worse than the Mafia, Katiana replied, still pissed that he was near Jayla's room.

Moms are deadly, just like a widow spider, when their babies are in trouble. We strike quickly; you will never see us coming.

Katiana, I knew you had some Mafia in you, Aiden smiled.

Make sure our baby is safe while they are out, Katrina told Giovanni.

We got our best men tailing them, and we have drone surveillance as a backup, Vanni replied.

That evening, before heading back to the house, we stopped by Alex's house to get his bags because we were leaving early in the morning to head to Disney World.

We started chilling, then got in his pool to cool off. Alex started kissing my neck, then he started playing with me. And we started getting into finally making out in the pool.

Alex gently leaned me up against the side of the pool. Every time Alex went inside me, he felt so amazing.

No one has ever made me moan like Alex did.

Alex made me feel things I've never felt before.

My legs felt weak like putty, experiencing making love as if for the very first time.

Afterwards, Alex and I took a shower, and he asked me if I was alright or if he had hurt me.

I told Alex that he didn't hurt me, but it was special to me because I knew that I truly loved him.

As we pulled off into traffic, going back to my house. We noticed the guard's car and waved at them. But a few cars down was a black SUV that passed by speeding.

Oh my God, I thought that it was Shane. Was he just watching me and Alex making love, crossed my mind?

Did Shane hear me moaning Alex's name as he was hitting my spot on the side of the pool?

Jayla, you alright? You look like something is on your mind, Alex asked me.

I replied, just thinking about the wonderful day we had.

When we pulled up to the house, I was afraid the guards were going to report what we did at Alex's house to my Dad or Uncle Aiden.

The one guy says that the last part won't be reported. I sighed in relief, and so did Alex, then we laughed.

The servants started loading the bags into the vehicles. I kissed Alex again and thanked him for the best afternoon ever.

We walked in the front door and were greeted by my grandparents.

Early that next morning, we got into different vehicles and headed to the airport, and started boarding Dad's plane.

We had breakfast on the plane, and it was good and plentiful. Alex sat down next to me, of course, and we were talking about last night.

We picked up my aunt Kelani and Zander in Vegas before we headed to Florida. I saw my auntie's baby bump and touched her tummy. I noticed that smile on her face; she was truly glowing, as the old saying goes.

We landed in Florida, got checked in, and did some sightseeing. That night, at dinner, we sat down and waited for our food. Zander seemed preoccupied or nervous.

After dinner, Zander suggested that they all take a walk down the street to work off dinner. The electric light show begins shortly afterwards. It's so full of bright colors, and it lights up the sky.

As we were watching the show, we noticed Minnie Mouse had come over to rub my aunt Kelani's belly. Then we noticed Mickey Mouse had come over and handed Zander something in his hand. Perhaps a small box of something? We all grabbed our mouths as Zander got down on one knee.

Zander then took Kelani's hand and began proposing, asking her to marry him.

We could not believe it; we were all shocked, no clue.

Grandma Ida and Mommy started crying. Kelani replied with tears as well. Yes, Zander, of course, I will marry you.

Tomorrow we're going shopping for some last-minute Christmas items, Katiana tells us. And then we talked about the surprise marriage proposal Zander sprang on us.

We had no idea that was going to happen, but it made this Christmas vacation even more special, Ida replied, still smiling.

My grandma, Ida, and Mom were talking to my auntie about different things. What colors and months would be great for getting married?

All I could do was think about how to sneak off and make love to Alex. I was happy for my aunt and Zander, but Alex was on my mind only.

All I can do is replay the first time we made love in the pool?

Alex was so gentle, and then he became like a crazed animal.

Alex found spots on me that I didn't know I had or existed.

We went back to the Disney World Resort directly across from the park to get some things started. We started to decorate for Christmas, singing Christmas carols, Grandma Ida and Mom were making cookies, and that's when Zander finally told us where we were going to spend our New Year's Eve. We were all shocked when he said *Tahiti*.

During our stay in Florida, the guys all went to the Disney Magnolia Golf Course to get some golfing in and have some male bonding time. "Get away from us girls," Mom said.

We did some shopping at Disney Springs, but we hadn't noticed that we were in there for two hours. Then we went into a local marketplace that had food, where we grabbed a mid-day snack. Aunt Kelani was hungry. Afterwards, we went to a place called the Orlando Vineland Premium Outlet. We spent four hours just looking at all kinds of things, including baby items.

Disney character–themed items were our main target. Mommy called Dad and told him to meet us back at the resort so they could wash up and get ready for dinner.

We ate dinner at a place called the Rose and Crown Dining Room. The next evening, we dined at a place called the Garden Grill. My aunt Kelani was craving a certain dish, and only that place served what she wanted. To be honest, she didn't give us time to look around for any other options—and Zander did not want to upset her or feel her wrath. If my aunt didn't eat when she wanted to, we all caught her wrath.

The very next day, we all attended a show called Drawn to Life. The whole family loved it and had an amazing time. The performers wore bright, beautiful costumes, which made it even more intriguing to watch.

Alex reached down and held my hand as we continued to watch the show. I'm so in love with Alex, I thought, smiling.

After we got back, Alex and I found a way to sneak off to fool around, just to be alone with each other and not with my family. Alex made me feel so different from Shane—not that I was comparing. The way Alex caressed my breast as he sucked on my nipples made me want to climb the walls for sure. Then the way he played with me, drawing low moans from my mouth, left me in ecstasy. Whenever Alex was close, it happened.

He made me orgasm back-to-back. It was draining, but I loved it.

Before the family left for Tahiti, we decided to take a trip to SeaWorld. Let me tell you—that day was off the hook! The family had so much fun, and we took so many pictures. I didn't know what made me feel like a kid in a candy store—looking at all the whales, riding the different rides, or having fun in the mirror house with Alex.

Or perhaps seeing the dolphin show and the dolphin splashed Giovanni, Zander, Uncle Aiden, and Alex? We laughed so hard.

Grandma Ida and Grandpa Vince enjoyed watching the other shows alone. The fact that we were listening to all the information and learning things. Not having our phones and just enjoying family time made my parents happy.

I glanced over and saw Zander rubbing Aunt Kelani's belly. She was starting to show, and his imagination grew as well. Thinking he was finally going to be a father, Zander was excited. The family was thrilled as well.

But we also enjoyed looking at all the Christmas decorations and watching live shows as we walked around. It just made Christmas even more exciting, seeing the decorations and everyone in a great mood.

We ate at the Flying Fish, but Aunt Kelani had to find something other than fish because it was not good to eat a lot of fish during pregnancy.

We stayed up late that night putting our presents out so the family could open them in the morning. That night, we had a good old-fashioned Christmas carol sing-along.

My auntie's older kids were there as well, and I know that made her very happy. Because she's not able to spend time with her grandkids and older kids often? And share her new growing family with them?

It was the first time I saw my auntie keep smiling, and she knew that her kids were not on board with getting pregnant at her age.

But they changed their minds once they saw how happy she was and that she was very happy with her new life with Zander.

Although she did not often discuss her past, Aunt Kelani said she would always love her ex. But she is much happier that she gave her new life a chance with Zander?

Alex held me in his arms and then leaned down to kiss my forehead. Mommy and Uncle Aiden looked at me and Alex in the corner. And knew that my feelings for Alex were serious. Besides, everyone in the family liked him.

Alex asked me to go take a walk with him to be alone. No one even knew we had sneaked off, nor looked for us?

So I assumed, but Mommy, Grandma Ida, and Aunt Kelani did? But they acted like they did not see me and Alex leave, but they peeped us trying to sneak out?

Alex and I walked along the beach holding hands and, on occasion, kissed. We knew security was around, but they did not make their presence known.

As we were walking along the beach, we came across some big rocks. We sat on them and watched the waves come up and roll back into the sea.

Alex kissed my neck, and that's all it took to get me started. I loved how Alex made me feel. Alex had me backed up against the wall when he lifted my dress, opened up my legs, and went inside me.

Alex feels so good inside me? I felt every inch of Alex going in and out. Making me moan, and the more I moaned. The harder Alex pumped faster, making me climax.

As we were walking back, we noticed my aunt's blind and balcony door was slightly open. We saw her and Zander having sex. The balcony door was open, so we could hear them, and I just looked at Alex with a shocked look.

Alex looked at me and smiled, as if nothing was happening. I looked at Alex with an expression of embarrassment. Then I thought? Guess they were thinking what we were thinking came to mind?

Now my next thought was, does Zander make my aunt feel the way Alex makes me feel? But why was I thinking that?

I can see why my aunt loved Zander so much. Wow, your aunt sounded like you did a few minutes ago, Alex said with a straight face. If Zander makes my aunt feel the way Alex makes me feel. No wonder she left her old life and moved to Vegas came to mind?

There was one missed call on my phone from Dayonna and Kirk wishing us a Merry Christmas and a Happy New Year.

We kissed goodnight, each took a shower, and were asleep in no time.

The next morning, we were all up super early. Exchanging and opening up gifts from the family.

I noticed my aunt and Zander. All I could do was smile at them. Trying not to be embarrassed about what Alex and I heard last night? They smiled back. I hope they never find out that we heard them. I whispered to Alex? Alex says you're overreacting, just act normal, he says?

It's normal, Alex told me? But it was my aunt and soon-to-be uncle having sex, I replied. So it makes me feel weird, I replied.

It's a part of our normal lives, Alex said to me. But it's different when it's dealing with your family, I replied.

That's like when I overheard my parents having sex? I had to put on my headphones; they were loud.

My cousins won't be joining us in Tahiti for New Year's. So later on today, Dad's pilot will take them back to Maryland.

My aunt looks so sad, but she was excited they spend a little time with them during Christmas.

So we kissed them all goodbye and told them to keep in touch.

Aunt Kelani cried as they watched them board the plane. Zander held my auntie in his arms as she watched them leave and cry more, watching the plane disappear out of sight.

Once the pilot returns, we'll start making our way towards Tahiti.

"Dad, how long our flight will take, I asked.

Mommy answered, about eleven hours and thirty-one minutes? Give or take, Mommy replied.

What are we supposed to do during that flight, I said.

You will have movies to watch or play games on the computer, Daddy replied. There is a whole bunch of other stuff to do on the plane, Blue Jay, Mommy answered as she packed.

The best part about my Dad having his own plane is that we can do or have anything we want, unlike other planes.

While we were on holiday, my Dad and uncle Aiden were also keeping close tabs on Arturo's location. And they get updates on a regular basis from someone.

One time, we overheard my Dad or uncle Aiden cussing. And whoever was on the other end told them to follow close to Arturo as if they were his underwear?

I didn't want to laugh because he is a dangerous man. But that shit was funny as hell, not sure who said it.

Aiden was talking to Zander about his business in Vegas while Aunt Kelani was sound asleep. Zander was rubbing her belly and then would kiss it. Zander was still talking to Aiden as he would sneak peeks at my Mom.

Mom and Uncle Aiden's eyes met each other a few times. I can see that my Mom still cares, maybe even loves my uncle Aiden. But won't cheat on my dad to keep the peace? At least I hope not, but looking at them makes me second-guess.

I then started looking out the window to think about something else besides my mom and Uncle Aiden. I could see the clouds and the sun setting in the sky as it started getting dark. The colors were so beautiful and vivid, with oranges and reds mostly standing out.

I took a few pictures to remember it, and maybe draw it. Throughout our Christmas holiday. We have taken so many pictures of the family. Then I could put them in the family album after making some copies for others to enjoy as well?

My plan was to make my aunt Kelani's album special by placing the pictures of her kids and grandkids together, along with Zander. So she can see the pictures of them, remember how they were enjoying each other, was my plan? Whenever my aunt is not around, she will have that to look at with Zander. It's not often they come to visit her, but she now has pictures of them to look at and put in the house in Vegas with Zander.

But no one noticed that Mom and Grandma Ida were also taking family pictures; they caught a few of me and Alex. I didn't notice, but she said to put it up in the house and our family album.

Alex and I started playing a game of Scrabble. That's when Zander and Aunt Kelani decided to team up and started playing a couples' against couples Scrabble game with us. To keep our minds away from being on the plane, and it worked for a while, until my aunt got hungry.

We stuffed our faces with pepperoni pizza, chips and salsa, and guacamole. And any other things that we could stuff our faces with.

Then, for the last five hours on the plane. We watched a movie, but then we began watching my aunt go back and forth to the bathroom.

We are so grateful that there are three bathrooms on this plane. They are much bigger than the other planes, and there's a place to take a private nap. Especially for the noisy people, not mentioning any names, my grandpa Vince? We asked my grandpa, Vince, to go into the back because he was making it hard to hear the music or the movie with his loud snoring. My grandma told him that he sounded like a trapped elephant. We laughed so hard, then he said. Ida, you don't snore at all? My grandma said, No, I don't and if I did. I would not sound like a buzz saw like you. My Dad just put his head down, trying not to be seen laughing. My uncle Aiden just shook his head and laughed as he read his paper. But it was so funny hearing my grandparents discussing with each other; they were more entertaining than the game at times. That's why we stopped playing and watched my grandparents go at it. They sounded like a bunch of middle school kids. Mommy says Control your Dad. Daddy replied Control your Mom. Then they started going back and forth. Uncle Aiden looked around at the newspaper and shook his head, saying, "Now look at the other kids." Then I said, 'Do I have to separate you four?' They looked at me, and Dad said Now we are getting scolded by our own child? How embarrassing Mommy said, then they all laughed.

Chapter 5:
New Year in Paradise on Earth

Good Morning, and welcome to The Moana Tahiti Resort. The resort is breathtaking, I had to admit. We are near the sea edge and also close to the land. So Mom suggested that after we take our bags to our rooms and chill? We decided to relax next to the Infinity pool to watch the sunset over the Island of Moorea. When we first arrived, it was raining, but it soon stopped as we checked in. And it remained hot and humid even after the rain? We spent our first day relaxing on the beach, taking occasional swims on the pure white sand. We're just enjoying ourselves and the water. My grandparents were lounging on their chairs in the crystal-clear blue water. Later that night, we watched the humpback whales in the distance from our balcony. Jumping in and out of the water. It was exciting to watch them while the sun started to set, and it looked as if they were touching the now-falling sky. All the colors popped and looked just like a painting. So I had to take a picture as I was taking pictures of the sunset. I caught one of my aunts and Zander holding hands on the beach. Then caught one as Zander got down on one knee and kissed her stomach? Then they continued to walk along the beach, still holding hands like two teenagers in love. Once we all got cleaned up. We decided just to go downstairs and have dinner at the Taapuna Restaurant tonight. We sat outside, looking out over the white-sanded beach as the palm trees swayed back and forth. Smelling the fresh sea air and just taking in the beautiful sight. The island's food was so delicious and filling.

The next day, after having breakfast, Zander had us go on a boat. We could see the humpback whales up close. At the same time, looking out the back of the boat.

Where are we going tomorrow, Vince asked Zander.

The next place we are going was decided by Kelani and Zander, Uncle Aiden replied, not looking up from the side of the boat.

So, where are we going, Vince then asked Aiden.

It's called the Water Garden of Vaipahi, Aiden replied.

That's where the beautiful plants and bright tropical-colored flowers grow, my Mom replied, smiling.

That would be the place, Zander replied, surprised that my Mom knew about that place.

I couldn't wait to see the botanical gardens located at the base of the mountain, Mommy says. Maybe we can hike the trail, Mommy says, forgetting about Auntie being pregnant. It's about a half-hour flat walk my grandma replied as she read the pamphlet.

Zander, can you see me walking up a mountain, Aunt Kelani says.

Zander tells my aunt, we can walk slowly if you want to Zander replied.

Hi, Grandma Ida and Grandpa Vince. Are you two alright to hike? I asked them. If we are not in a rush, I'm

Good, she told me. Us old birds will be fine, Grandpa Vince said. Grandma Ida rolled her eyes, and I laughed.

Speak for yourself, Vince, Grandma Ida replied. I'm not old, I'm in my prime.

We all laughed, only my grandma would say something like that.

Momma, are you and Vince going to be alright? My auntie had asked them again?

Yes, Kelani, are you going to be alright is the question grandma asked.

Ke, are you alright for the hike? I mean, being pregnant, Zander asked.

Zander, we are not in a race; we are walking. Besides, it's good exercise. We will take it nice and slow; Zander told Kelani as he kissed her. I love you, Zander, my Prince, my aunt replied.

Before we began hiking up the mountain, we all put on some comfortable shoes and light clothes. It's very humid here, Giovanni replied. Even though it rained, it just made it hotter, Daddy said as the driver pulled up. We saw some beautiful, bright, neon pink flowers. Mommy was then telling us about them. We started snapping pictures. Once we got out, we made our way to the mountain entrance. We saw some roosters, some ducks, both big and small. One came near Alex, trying to bite him? I told him to give him some of the breadcrumbs that we got at the entrance. Dad and Grandpa took some pictures along the pond. Then we saw another pond full of tropical-looking flowers. And you could see all the lily pads in the water as I snapped pictures, looking in amazement. The grass was so green, and it felt so nice on my bare feet. While walking the trails, we noticed a lot of different plants. Then we saw the waterfalls and felt the water.

There was so much to take in; I told my Mom. This place was amazing, full of different colors, looked like a majestic garden, my grandma, Ida, said. As we went further into the garden, we noticed these big statues that looked like giants. So, of course, we had to take pictures. We sat along the waterfall to catch our breath and to let my aunt and grandparents rest. I went up close to see the flowers and took in their natural beauty. Mommy loves bright colors just as much as I do. We were just like kids on Christmas morning, taking in all the natural beauty of the garden.

As we started walking back to the van. We came across a souvenir shop and picked up a souvenir. We got a snack to hold us until we go eat? We got something to drink to quench our thirst while walking back to the van that we saw in the distance. It was hot and we wanted to stay hydrated.

Did you enjoy this spot, Zander asked us. Mommy answered, she sure did, and wanted to go back.

I have to say, Alex and I also enjoyed it, I replied to Zander. I loved getting up close and personal with nature, my Dad replied.

However, before we left, Aunt Kelani had to make a pit stop to relieve herself. You gotta love being pregnant, Mommy being sarcastic? Always going to the bathroom. We just laughed, then when my auntie came out, she asked everyone. What was so funny?

I looked over and caught my uncle Aiden looking at Daddy as he put a bright pink flower in Mom's hair.

When we got back we decided to try some place down the street called Meherio Tahitian Bistro? We knew that New Year's Eve would be here in a few days. We needed to ask around to see what they do on that day over there.

As we were eating, the waitress began to talk to my Dad. Overheard you wanting to know what we do on New Year's, she replied?

She then told my Dad about a place called Christmas Island. And it's on the waterfront Esplanade, and at midnight, there are fireworks displayed?

So my Dad wanted to know more, and he talked to her more. And then my Dad talked to a man, and the next thing out of his mouth was. We are all set for New Year's Eve, my Dad said as he smiled.

When we got back to our rooms, Aunt Kelani and Zander went straight back to their room. Aunt Kelani said she was drained, which made Zander worry. If we overdid it? But my aunt told Zander she wanted to take in all that we explored.

My grandparents sat outside drinking a beer while overlooking the sea. Enjoying the sea smells, talking about the trip so far? Talking about what we did and what we hope to do?

Aiden told Giovanni he was going to check on any updates about Arturo.

Daddy and Mommy took a walk along the beach holding each other's hands. I noticed my uncle looking at them while drinking a beer. Uncle Aiden has to be lonely, I thought to myself.

How come your uncle Aiden isn't dating anyone, Alex asked me. else?

Good question, I replied to Alex, it's not like he's ugly? My uncle could have any woman out here, I reply.

We also decided to walk along the beach and enjoy some alone time. Watching the beautiful sunsets along the sea. It was breathtaking, and then we shared a kiss. Being alone on the beach, we decided to make love under the night sky. And between smelling the sea and hearing the crash of the waves, we had a magical sexual encounter on the beach.

Making love to Alex is different every time. From the way he cups my breast to how he goes deep inside my body? Alex never feels the same; it's like making love to another person every time. And Alex always makes me want to scream just by touching me a certain way.

On our way back to the room, I noticed my uncle Aiden was holding something in his hand that made him emotional. Perhaps a picture of him and my mom comes to mind?

What happened, Uncle Aiden kept saying as he drank from the cup. God, why did you make me lose my only true love? He says.

Uncle Aiden is clearly drinking something stronger than water to get out his feelings about his past with my mom.

Then my grandpa Vince was talking to him, trying to calm him down? Grandpa Vince could see that something or someone had uncle Aiden in his feelings. Was he still in love with my Mom after all these years and didn't want to hurt my Dad or me, I wondered?

Aiden never stopped Katiana, but won't act on it? He made a promise to himself not to indulge because he loved and respected his big brother's marriage. So he would have to try to hide his true feelings for Katiana?

Vince hugged Aiden and told him to sleep it off. Part of me felt so sorry watching her uncle clearly in pain. As I wondered, was I right about my uncle still being in love with her Mom?

The next day, Uncle Aiden didn't join us on our outing. He had joined us for breakfast, but quickly made up some excuse and then left. Grandpa Vince looked worried but understood, and in a way, so did I.

We went to the Museum of Tahiti and the island. As we first started pulling off, I noticed Uncle Aiden sitting by the palm trees with a drink in his hands. And my heart sank thinking we were leaving him alone?

When we finally pulled up to the museum. We noticed these five statues and their colors caught my eye. As we began walking around, we started seeing different statues inside glass cases and found out where they were from. Then we saw some old guns displayed in a weird case. Next to it was a boat inside a shattered glass case. The artifacts were intriguing, but it was also nice to see where they found them. I love learning about history, just like my soon-to-be uncle Zander. But my other family members are not so much?

The rest of the family went outside as Alex and I brought some souvenirs to take home. As we walked out, we noticed the family was looking at the natives dancing and singing songs in their native language, which seemed very interesting.

Zander hugged Aunt Kelani as they watched the performers. We could see the happiness that my aunt felt whenever they are near each other. We all enjoyed the songs as well as their dancing. Even though we didn't understand the words, we knew it was clearly telling a story of love, and it was sad. The rhythm of the beats would change, and it made us dance along.

I called my uncle Aiden and asked if he would meet us at the Tahiti La Plage to have dinner with the family.

So as we pulled up, Dad noticed Uncle Aiden. When he got out, he gave him a hug. And said I'm glad you showed up. We missed you. Which was true, it was weird not seeing my uncle.

As Mommy got out of the car, she caught him looking at her. They made eye contact. And I knew he really did it for her came to my mind.

We all got seated and looked at the menu. Then I excused myself to go to the bathroom. Must have been something I ate because I got sick?

Our table was outside under the coconut tree, and when we took our shoes off. You could feel how soft the white sand under your feet was. Dining under the warm night sky, looking out at the sea, was the most relaxing feeling.

As I was walking back from the restroom for the second time. I noticed my uncle Aiden in the lobby and gave him a hug. Then whispered, Glad you came, in his ear. He smiled.

Uncle Aiden kissed me and asked me if I was feeling okay.

I think I ate too much earlier, but I feel better now, I replied.

We enjoyed dinner and talked about New Year's Eve.

Don't forget tomorrow we're going to Christmas Island, Giovanni replied excitedly.

So after we ate, we all turned in early to prepare for tomorrow's trip, or so I thought. When I opened my door to go out. I overheard my Daddy and uncle talking about Arturo and where he was last seen.

Uncle Aiden was telling Giovanni that he was last seen in Florida.

What quickly came to my mind was hope Shane didn't see Alex and me having sex on the beach? I didn't need a crazy man following me? It gave me anxiety just thinking about Shane. Besides, I don't even know if Shane really liked having sex with me or faked it. I mean, Shane is older than me, and I'm sure he has had his fill of women over the years.

I woke up around two and couldn't sleep thinking about earlier. I glanced outside my balcony door and noticed two figures. I noticed two people, but couldn't see who they were. Whoever it was, they were getting up from behind the palm tree line?

I can only imagine what had just happened to me and laughed. Then

I lay back down until morning.

That next morning, before we left, we had breakfast at the Concept Grill. We grabbed something, quickly got our bags, and headed for the boat. It would be a couple of hours before we got to the island. Besides, we wanted to do some sightseeing before the New Year activities began if we got there earlier than expected.

Before we took off, I noticed Mom and Grandma were having a seriously heated conversation. I overheard Mom saying to my Grandma. I never stopped loving him, and I will take that secret to the grave.

What secret could Mom be keeping from the family now, I wondered? What don't we know about the family? Or is it something that I should know about that comes instantly to my mind?

I guess if it's important, hopefully Mom would tell me? Besides, Mom told me she would tell me anything I wanted to know if I asked her.

On the boat, Alex and I looked at the whales jumping in the distance. Then Zander and Uncle Aiden joined in as well. As we were looking at them, Aunt Kelani started feeling unwell, possibly from the boat ride. Zander quickly rushed by her side to see if she wanted to sit down.

The woman, Dr., on the boat gave my aunt something to help with nausea and told her and Zander it wouldn't hurt the baby.

Grandpa Vince started talking to Uncle Aiden once Zander left. Mommy and Daddy were also looking at the water as they held hands. Grandma Ida noticed Uncle Aiden looking at Mommy as he drank his drink. And Grandma just quickly looked away?

Grandma Ida knew Mom still loved Uncle Aiden, that's what I was thinking.

As we were pulling up to the dock, a sign said, Welcome to Christmas Island. Yay, we are finally here, I yelled.

As we started getting out, we started walking towards a resort. Is that where we're staying, Mom asked Daddy? He answered, yes, this is where we would be staying. "He wanted to get checked in and wait for tonight's festivities.

We got checked in and wanted to walk around, but my grandparents decided to rest up for tonight instead. So did my parents, or did they want to enjoy themselves? But I know I just wanted some alone time with Alex.

That evening, we were all looking for something colorful to wear for the New Year's festivities. All day, we heard from my auntie telling Zander. This doesn't fit around my stomach, this one is too tight around my breast, and we didn't want to laugh.

Zander told my aunt that no matter what she wears, she was always going to be beautiful in his eyes.

Two hours to showtime, Daddy yelled. Maybe we should start making our way to the beach. Hope you picked out a good spot to watch the show, Grandpa Vince says.

As we finally started heading to a spot. My Dad got approached by someone who told him something? Dad looked at us and said that we were all set up. Dad then explained that we are in a tent with comfortable chairs by the water for tonight's events.

We began walking over near our setup, which was phenomenal. Bright colored and festive decorations to get us ready for New Year's Eve. We sat down and began to eat the food in our tent. There's so much food to choose from, Grandma Ida replied, looking around in amazement.

Daddy said that I could have a drink tonight, but don't overdo it. I was shocked.

The black sand seemed to sparkle in the sun that was beginning to set. Moonlight dining under the stars was Beautiful. And the water was so clear and blue. Noticed some people on the beach, some were in the water enjoying a night swim.

The countdown began, we started counting down as well, 4, 3, 2, 1 Happy New Year! Everyone kissed their loved ones. Grandma Ida kissed Grandpa Vince on the cheek, which shocked all of us. Mommy kissed Daddy, of course, Zander kissed Aunt Kelani, and I kissed my Alex.

Then I walked over and gave my uncle Aiden a kiss on the cheek. We then all watched the fireworks as they lit up the night sky for an hour or more.

Next, we looked and saw the waterfall in front of us turning different colors as the music played in the background. Looking at all the beautiful colors was simply magnificent.

We got back to the room finally around two because it began to rain. Daddy was so drunk that Uncle Aiden and Grandpa had to help him back into the room.

Alex and I stayed up simply enjoying the fantastic scenery. We saw my grandparents go into their room, still talking about tonight's festivities. Aunt Kelani and Zander went back to their room. Zander was helping my auntie; she was tired from the whole day and needed to rest.

As Alex and I were talking, I noticed Mommy talking to Uncle Aiden, but I turned my attention back to Alex. We decided to turn in because we had gotten sleepy and decided to go to bed. I got up to use the restroom when I heard someone come in the front door. Was it my Mom? Why is she coming in the front door at this time, I wonder? I didn't say anything. Besides, she's my Mom, not my business.

The next morning, the whole family met and had breakfast at Tahiti La Plage on the white sand overlooking the sea.

Good morning, everyone, Dad said, still hungover. Hope everyone enjoyed last night on the beach. It was breathtaking and spectacular, Grandma Ida replied.

Blue Jay, sorry you had to see your Dad that way. But we were having so much fun enjoying family, and that meant a lot to him, Daddy replied.

We have our lovely daughter back in our lives, Daddy says, and most importantly, his baby brother Aiden back in his life. We have three new family additions to the family as well, Vince replied. I'm very blessed to have the family I have, Daddy said, getting teary-eyed.

I noticed Mom and Uncle Aiden hardly looked at each other as we boarded the plane.

I'm not the only one to notice, I thought? Grandma Ida didn't say anything, but the look on her face as she sat down and analyzed those two spoke loud and clear. The situation between my Mom and uncle had changed, but how?

Goodbye, Tahiti, until the next time we are able to come visit you again, Dad said, looking out the window.

The ride home was quiet, I guess, because we were all tired. I started dozing off, but noticed Mom and Uncle Aiden locking eyes as if they were having a private connection just between them two.

What happened on that last night on the island, and why were Mommy and Uncle Aiden acting so strangely towards each other, I wondered? And how they are acting now, I wondered, as I saw Mom coming in the front door of our villa at five this morning.

But I assumed Mom went to bed after we got back? After all, Alex and I went to bed around three thirty, but then I noticed Mommy. Which had to be around five or five-thirty, so clearly Mom didn't go to bed as I thought.

But the last time I remembered seeing Mommy, she was talking to Uncle Aiden? It was around two fifteen then, but I finally lay down closer to three?

Why am I trying to think about this anyway? I think to myself. My head shouldn't be imagining what I'm thinking now?

I'm so glad no one sees what I'm thinking right now. Everything about last night was phenomenal and memorable in every way. This whole holiday getaway has been very incredible and well deserved, I'm thinking.

We first dropped off Zander and Aunt Kelani back in Vegas, then we made our way back home. Alex and I kissed each other goodnight and decided to make plans to meet up tomorrow.

My grandparents will come back on this plane later this week. Mr. Stan met Dad and Uncle Aiden coming out of his office door.

I need to fill you both in about the new information on Arturo once you two get settled, Stan said.

Daddy and Uncle Aiden's expressions turned serious, and both nodded at Mr. Stan.

Chapter 6:
It's Positive, but who is it

Alex and I have gotten closer and have been having sex on a regular basis since Christmas vacation.

Dayonna and Kirk came for a visit the week after we got back from Tahiti. I showed Dayonna all the wonderful pictures and videos we had taken on the trip. Alex and I, as well, had brought Dayonna and Kirk back some souvenirs from every spot we visited.

Alex and Kirk went outside to talk and catch up with each other, and we did the same. Dayonna began telling me she had some news to share.

I finally took my relationship to the next level with Kirk, Dayonna tells me.

I then shared something with her. I've been having sex with Alex regularly, I replied, smiling.

Since they were not going to be in town long, only for the weekend because of their school schedules, we decided to go and have dinner in town to catch up.

While at dinner, I had to excuse myself to the restroom because I was feeling sick. I came back out to the table and kept it to myself that I threw up.

Later that night, after we came back from dinner. I noticed Mom coming from the bathroom near the living room, looking flushed.

Mommy, we're back, I said. Are you feeling alright? You look a bit pale, I told her.

Think it was the island and the heat playing games with me, Mom replied. I'm glad you had fun with Dayonna she says, looking sick. Are they settled in the guest house, Mom asked, walking towards the kitchen.

I'm going to get some ginger ale and wait for your Dad on the couch to come back from the Country Club. He's with your uncle, Mom said, drinking her soda. Which really meant in code they were going to the Mafia headquarters and talk about business.

Hope you feel better, Mom, I said before heading to my room.

"Thank you, Jayla baby. Did you want to talk about something you looked worried about, Mom asked me.

No, just tired from last week, I guess,I replied, going to bed..

Okay, night, my Blue Jay, Mom replied after a kiss on my cheek.

I started undressing when I heard a noise coming from my window. I peeked out and saw the guards walking the grounds.

Mr. Stan saw me peeking, and I waved to him. Mr. Stan waved back.

So I heard another sound but didn't bother to get up, assuming it was Mr. Stan again.

But the next morning at breakfast, one of the security guards showed my Dad the camera footage from last night. It showed Mr. Stan waving to me, but it also showed someone else looking at me through my window minutes later, not Mr. Stan? Clearly watching me as I slept, but who, I wonder.

Dad can't see a clear image of the person, and it was too big to be my ex-boyfriend Shane. Unless Shane gained weight, Giovanni thought? I haven't seen Shane in a couple of months, so I really don't know if it's possible.

But then I thought he wouldn't be the type of guy to watch me sleep. Let's just hope that it wasn't him who didn't watch me and Alex having sex in my room the other night?

Mommy called Aunt Kelani to see how she was doing. Aunt Kelani then shared some shocking news with Mom. After her visit, they discovered she was pregnant with twins.

Mom motioned for me to come into the living room and shared the news with me about Aunt Kelani. I got on the phone and said so you're having twins?

How is Zander taking the news? "I asked." Is he excited?

Zander is super excited, she told me and Mom. Can't wait to see what the sexes are, Mom says as she continues to talk to my auntie.

I'm so happy for them, Mom says. Is Kelani finally giving Zander what she thought she couldn't have?

That night, before dinner, I overheard Mommy asking Daddy to keep a secret. Something must have happened long ago, but what, I said to myself, trying not to get caught, still listening?

Maybe if he knew what I saw, maybe it would have been a different outcome she yelled at my Dad.

What would have been different, and what did Mommy see years ago, I wondered?

I quickly moved away from the door as my parents came towards the cracked door. But Mom was now full of tears and headed straight to their room, slamming the door.

Later that evening, Alex came over and joined us for dinner in the family room. Now my parents seemed like they were back in love. Like nothing ever happened?

So I didn't worry about what I heard earlier; clearly, I worked it out, I thought.

Aiden, can I see you for a minute in the office, Daddy said. Stan has discovered some new information about Arturo.

Is Katiana feeling well? Aiden asked Giovanni. She looked a bit pale,

Uncle Aiden said, looking at her.

I think she's coming down with something, perhaps the flu, Giovanni replied. Perhaps Aiden says under his breath, but looks puzzled.

Blue Jay, are you getting sick also? You look a bit pale as well, Uncle Aiden said. You're looking pale like your Mom, Uncle Aiden replied.

Maybe I will have the doctor stop by and give my two girls a check-up, Daddy said, walking to his office. Then told me to go to my room and rest.

The next day, Uncle Aiden went on about his normal day when he stopped in the hallway bathroom to wash his hands. As Aiden got ready to throw his paper towel away, he noticed two pregnancy tests. Those were clearly pink, indicating a positive pregnancy, but who?

Aiden's eyes widened in surprise as he thought to himself who could it be? But there are six women in the house, and only five were still able to get pregnant to Aiden's knowledge.

Giovanni, who was standing nearby, noticed what Aiden was looking at and reacted. Giovanni raised an eyebrow. Who is the lucky person he asked, Aiden? Aiden shakes his head, not having a word to say, and just have a shocked look on his face.

Aiden's mind started racing with possibilities of who it could be, but he wondered if he was overreacting. Was it Katiana or maybe Jayla? The suspense was killing Aiden, and he couldn't wait to find out who the expectant mother or mothers were.

Chapter 7:
A Wedding, Baby, and Other Scenarios

Dad walked out in a daze and waited for Aiden to come into his office for an update about Arturo. Later, when Giovanni went back into the bathroom, he didn't see the trash bag from earlier; it was gone.

Giovanni began to think if he really saw the test at all, because he had been drinking. Zander and Kelani were getting married in a few weeks, and my mom and I had to get some dresses made for the special occasion.

Mom made a strange comment as we were getting fitted for our dresses: "If you need to talk to me about anything, you can." I looked puzzled and remembered the plane ride back, how Mom and Uncle Aiden acted differently towards each other. So then I replied, "You can talk to me about anything too."

Not knowing that when I went to the bathroom earlier, I noticed the pregnancy test. I automatically thought it was Mom's. She had been sick and different since they returned from Tahiti, I thought. Maybe Mom didn't know how to tell us yet, I thought.

But what I didn't know was that after I used the bathroom, her Mom came in after her and saw the test, thinking that I was pregnant and afraid to tell them, well, her Dad mostly.

So I got a new bag and took the trash bag out so that Dad or Uncle Aiden wouldn't find it. But I was too late; my Dad and Uncle had already seen it.

So Mom finally came out and asked me if I was pregnant. I asked my Mom, "Are you pregnant, Mommy?" Before either one of us could answer the question, the doorbell rang. "Mr. Alex is here to see you, Ms. Jayla. And dinner is nearly ready," Ms. Gracie told us.

So no one said anything else, just looking and smiling at each other. I gave Alex a big hug and a kiss on the lips. Daddy shook Alex's hand, and my Uncle Aiden did as well.

We began talking about the upcoming wedding between Zander and Aunt Kelani. Alex and I were trying to coordinate our outfits. Then Dad asked Alex, "How serious are you about being with Jayla?"

Alex replied to my Dad and Uncle Aiden, who were listening closely, "I love her, and someday I plan to marry her and stay in the family business as well." Mommy said, "Welcome to the family, Alex. We love you and your brother like family."

When we were done with dinner, my parents asked Alex a question that really surprised me. They asked Alex if he wanted to move in with them. Uncle Aiden replied, "You can be closer to Jayla," but it was to make it easier for them to keep an eye on him because of Arturo.

Alex told Giovanni and Aiden that it would be his pleasure to stay in the guest room until we got engaged. Alex was an old-fashioned guy in certain things, but I loved the idea that Alex would be closer to me.

Mommy quickly excused herself from the table and headed to the bathroom in the hall. Dad looked at Uncle Aiden and smirked, as if he had gotten an answer to the mystery pregnancy test. Uncle Aiden seemed to understand but didn't react.

When Mom came back to the table, Daddy asked if she was alright. "Never been better," Mommy replied, drinking her juice. That's when I thought maybe it was my Mom who was pregnant.

Later that night, the news of Alex moving in was just what I had been waiting for. I started feeling nauseous and tried to make sense of the test results. I had taken a test that day to see if I might be pregnant by Alex, but I wanted to see the doctor to make sure. And if Mom was also pregnant, she hadn't told my Dad yet. Maybe she wanted to do it herself, I thought.

I got ready for bed to rest and texted Alex: "Good night, my love, and can't wait to be closer to you." Alex replied, "Love you always, my Blue Jay, sweet dreams."

The very next week, Alex started moving into the guest house. Alex had already asked Dad for some additional things to be put in on his behalf, and between Daddy and Uncle Aiden, they made the additions happen for Alex.

That following week, Alex told me he would officially be all moved in, but they had to stop because it was my Aunt Kelani and Zander's wedding. The family was on their way to Vegas for the unisex bachelor/bachelorette party, and their wedding was the next day.

We were all starting to load into the car, but I forgot my one bag. So I ran upstairs to my room to get it. On my way back downstairs, I noticed Mom and Uncle Aiden kissing again as he rubbed her stomach.

Maybe Uncle Aiden was rubbing Mom's stomach because he wanted her to feel better? Or maybe Mom told Uncle Aiden that she was pregnant by Dad, and he wished them well? But why was he kissing Mom, I thought? I know they are close, I thought, so every time I see them talking, I have to learn not to jump to conclusions, I told myself.

"Are Grandma and Grandpa coming?" I asked Mommy when she finally got in the car. "They are already there," Mommy replied. "They arrived last night," Uncle Aiden added, saying he had talked to Grandpa Vince.

"Do you want a glass of wine, dear?" Daddy asked Mommy. "No, I think some ginger ale instead," Mommy replied. Dad kissed Mommy on her cheek. Mom looked shocked.

"What was that for?" Mommy asked Daddy, looking puzzled. "Just because I love you, sweetheart, no reason," Dad said. Uncle Aiden looked down at his computer, acting like he wasn't paying attention, but clearly saw the hurt in his eyes.

We finally arrived in Vegas a few hours later and started heading to the luggage claim, then went outside to catch a cab to our hotel destination. "Dad, where are we staying again?" I asked.

"It's called The Venetian, and we have to get a gondola ride," Dad replied. "It's just like you're in Italy," he said.

"Are you serious, Dad? There's real water in the hotel and a boat you can ride on?" I asked. "I've never been to Vegas," I said.

"Here comes our ride now," Dad said. "A limo, really Dad?" I asked. "A freaking limo," I said.

"Yes, what else did you expect? Go big or go home," Dad replied.

Dad's phone rang as we were getting in. "Oh, hello, Zander? Yeah, we just got in and we're heading to the hotel now," Dad answered. "We'll meet you and Kelani there in a few," Dad said.

As they drove past different places, I was mesmerized by the different sights. "Look at all these lights," I said. "Alex, look at all these different hotels," I said, tapping him to get his attention.

"Maybe we can stay over to see some sights," I asked Alex. This time, Alex and I were sharing a room. "Alex, do you realize we're sharing a room?" I said under my breath. "Had Dad realized that I was growing up?" I thought.

"I think your Dad realizes that you are growing up," Alex said. "I'll always be Daddy's baby girl, but I am growing up," I told Alex.

My parents had adjoining rooms to our room, but it was alright. We noticed my grandparents were on the opposite side of Uncle Aiden's room. "No one was adjoining my grandparents?" I thought.

"Uncle Aiden is on the other side of us," I told Alex. Alex replied, "Noted."

Alex said, "Then you have to be quiet when we're having sex; they might hear you," Alex whispered in my ear.

"Don't worry, the rooms are soundproof," Mom leaned in and said. We started laughing. "How would you know that exactly?" I asked her.

"Your uncle and I came here when we were dating for a concert," Mommy replied. "We stayed in the very room he's in," Mom said, laughing. "We'll talk more about that later, Blue Jay," Mom whispered in my ear and left.

As we were leaving for the bachelorette party, we were greeted by a familiar voice. "Hey, there!" the voice said. "We were looking for you guys," I said, smiling.

"Hi, Mom, Hi, Vince! How was your flight here to Vegas?" Mommy asked. "It was good," Ida told Mommy, looking at her tummy. "How was yours?" Grandma Ida asked Giovanni.

"It was raining, then it stopped. Now we can eat," Mommy said.

The host, Melvin, greeted us as we walked in. "Good evening, I'm Melvin. Are you part of the Zander and Kelani party?" he asked.

"Yes, we all are," Giovanni replied to Melvin. "Please follow me; I will take you to the room," Melvin said.

As they entered the party, it was beautifully decorated, and I was speechless. "Wow, look at this, you guys! This doesn't look like our lobby where we're staying at," I replied.

"May I ask where you're staying?" Melvin said.

"We are staying at the amazing Venetian hotel," Giovanni replied.

"Great place, but to answer your question, Miss, all of our hotels are decorated with different themes," Melvin explained.

Zander and Aunt Kelani greeted us, looking happy. "Hey, you guys made it finally," Zander said to us.

"How are you doing, Sis?" Mommy asked Aunt Kelani. "I feel like a whale," Kelani replied to Mommy, laughing.

"Zander, are you ready for the big day?" Uncle Aiden asked. "I am indeed, can't wait to see my beautiful fiancée walking down the aisle to me and saying our I-do's to one another, starting our new journey together," Zander replied.

The wedding rehearsal was about to begin, and we practiced the whole thing three times. After the second time, we had it down, I think. "I think they just wanted to practice the kissing part," I told Alex.

"I will be walking down the aisle with Alex, and Mom will be walking down with Uncle Aiden because Dad will be walking Aunt Kelani down the aisle," I explained.

As the night went on, my grandparents were asked to light the candle at the front of the church for tradition. Now that the rehearsal was over, they were ready to eat, have some drinks, and get ready for the wedding the next evening.

"The wedding is being held in the evening to catch some pictures with the famous Vegas sunset in the background," Zander said.

Alex and I slow-danced a lot during the party, enjoying each other's company. Alex whispered to me, "You realize we'll be alone, and we can make love all night?"

I just laughed at Alex. "You're so crazy, you know that." "Alex, look how happy my aunt and Zander look," I said. "Just as you will look on our wedding day," Alex replied.

"I love you, Alex, and I'm so glad we met in the lobby." "Tomorrow, my aunt will be Mrs. Kelani Zanay Ragan, famous author and wife of the famous entrepreneur of Vegas," I told Alex.

We finally said our goodbyes to Aunt Kelani and Zander.

Early the next day, all us girls would be meeting up at Kelani and Zander's house to get our makeup and hair done and get ready for the wedding there, along with Aunt Kelani. Meanwhile, Daddy, Alex, Uncle Aiden, and Zander would be getting dressed at his office.

Daddy had security at the wedding to make sure they didn't have any unexpected surprises. As they headed back to the hotel, Dad told Mom he had a few errands to run before tomorrow and for her to go back to the room.

Daddy kissed Mommy before she got out of the car. "Aiden, make sure everyone gets back to their rooms safely," Giovanni said.

"As you wish," Uncle Aiden replied. "Would you like me to come with you?" he asked Daddy.

"No, I'm fine, but we'll talk when I get back," Giovanni smiled.

I kissed my grandparents and then kissed Mom before we closed our door, prepping for the early morning. "Be up and ready by eight," Mom screamed through our door.

"Aiden, can I have a word with you?" Mommy asked him. "Let's go in my room," Aiden replied to Katiana. "It's double soundproof," Aiden said.

"You still have that hook-up," Katiana said, laughing. "You can say that," Aiden replied.

"I want to talk about our last night in Tahiti," Katiana said. "You don't have to say anything; it wasn't supposed to happen," Aiden said.

"Aiden, I'm still in love with you," Katiana burst out. "I never stopped loving you, Aiden," Katiana said, tearing up. "That night after we kissed, one thing led to another," Katiana said. "You kissed my neck so gently, and when we laid in the black sand, Aiden, I was so caught up. Then you began to go inside me; it felt just like old times," Katiana said.

"I've been thinking about you and that night ever since," Katiana told Aiden. "You're the only one who made me feel that way," Aiden told Katiana.

"Do you still feel a bit under the weather?" Aiden asked. "You didn't drink or eat much tonight," Aiden replied.

"You can say that I'm not feeling well," Katiana replied sarcastically. "This is for you," Katiana handed Aiden a piece of paper. "Don't open it until you're alone," Katiana said.

"We'll talk again soon, Aiden," Katiana said. "I want to make love to you, Katiana," Aiden told her. "I don't want Giovanni to have you tonight," Aiden whispered in Katiana's ear.

The next morning, Katiana crept back to her room. "Did Mommy spend the night in Uncle Aiden's room?" I wondered as I saw her creeping up the hallway.

"Jayla, God, you scared me," Alex said. "What are you doing in the hallway this early?" Alex asked me.

"I was just getting some ice for my juice that I brought back from the party," I quickly replied. "Well, you have to get a move on so you can meet your Mom and Grandmother in the lobby," Alex replied. "Yeah, so we can go to my aunt's house," I remembered.

"I'll see you later, beautiful," Alex said to me before I left. "You all right? What's on your mind?" Alex asked.

"I don't think my Dad came back to the room last night," I told Alex.

"Why do you say that?" Alex asked, sounding concerned.

But before I could say anything, Grandmother Ida pushed me toward the now-open elevator doors.

"You will see your handsome man later," Grandmother Ida said. "Hello Alex, goodbye Alex," she told him as the doors began to close.

"Hello, good morning, and goodbye, Ms. Ida," Alex replied, laughing.

"Good morning, Princess. Did you sleep well?" Mommy asked me.

"Yeah, like a log. What about you, Mommy?" I asked.

"Well, your dad finally showed up to the room around four," she replied. "I asked your dad where he was, and he said he was downstairs gambling."

Just then, the car pulled up in front of Zander's house, and we started walking to the front door. Zander was heading out but was kissing my aunt as we were about to knock.

"Good morning, ladies. I'm heading to my office," Zander said. "See you all at the church." Then he pulled off.

"Hey, Sis," Katiana said.

"We're here, Auntie. You excited about today?" I asked.

"Good morning. How are you feeling, Kelani?" Ida asked.

"I feel great," Kelani told her mom. "And I can't wait to say 'I do' to the love of my life. But my stomach feels like butterflies are in there," she mentioned to Mommy.

"Drink some ginger ale. It's that morning sickness getting to you," Ida told her.

"And I think I gained some weight," Kelani told Katiana.

"Don't say that, Kelani. Today is your wedding day," Ida reminded her.

"Well, Mommy, I think I have," Kelani replied. "Look."

"Ladies, are you ready for your wedding makeovers?" a woman asked.

"Katiana, are you feeling alright?" Kelani asked her. "I heard you in the bathroom."

Katiana just looked.

"Are you? Don't say anything. Kelani, promise me," Katiana

50

whispered.

"I need to make sure—and exactly how far along I am," Katiana told Kelani, holding her mouth in shock.

"That would be awesome if both of us were pregnant at the same time," Kelani said.

"It might be three of us that are pregnant," Katiana said sarcastically.

"No, Katiana, are you talking about our little Blue Jay?" Kelani asked, wondering. "Has she said anything to you?"

"So how do you think Giovanni will react?" Kelani asked.

"It might not be Giovanni's," Ida said.

"Katiana, whose baby is it?" Kelani asked. Ida whispered, "Perhaps its Aiden's."

"Katiana—oh my," Kelani said, not shocked.

"Today is all about you and Zander, not me," Katiana said. "I will get all this figured out soon."

"What are we figuring out?" I asked as I entered the room.

"Blue Jay, your mom might be pregnant," Ida said. "And are you pregnant, Blue Jay?" Grandmother Ida asked me.

"Damn, Ma, thanks for keeping it a secret," Katiana said.

"Our little Blue Jay might be in the family way," Ida smiled.

"She's not so little, Mom," Katiana replied.

"So, have you told Aiden yet?" Ida asked Katiana.

"Mom, what is Grandma Ida talking about?" I asked.

"I see how Aiden looks at you, Katiana. Are you still in love with him?" Ida asked under her breath. "But if you are, that's not my story to tell," she added.

"What's everyone looking at?" Kelani asked.

"Blue Jay, you would tell us if something was wrong, right?" Grandma asked me.

"Yeah, I guess so—or Mommy," I replied.

"We will talk tomorrow, alright ladies," Grandma Ida said. "Today it's about a wedding celebration for Zander and Kelani."

"You make a beautiful bride," I told my auntie.

"You do make a marvelous bride, sis," Mommy agreed.

"Zander will surely cry when he sees you come down the aisle,"

Grandma Ida said, tearing up.

"I'm so nervous and scared," Kelani replied to her.

"Our ride is here, ladies," Kelani said, looking out the front door.

"Alright, are we ready to go?" Katiana asked.

"Thank you for holding my dress up in the back, Aunt Kelani," I told her.

"My pleasure, and no problem. You look so beautiful," I said.

"I'm so very happy for you two," Grandma Ida told Aunt Kelani.

As we arrived at the church, I couldn't help but notice how packed it was. We went inside and waited for our cue to start down the aisle. "It's almost time to start walking down," one of the church ladies whispered.

As we began to line up, I noticed Alex in his tuxedo.

"You are looking very handsome, Alex," I said to him.

"And you are looking pretty beautiful yourself, Blue Jay," Alex replied.

As we began to walk down the aisle, I couldn't help but notice the full church. Family and friends had come from everywhere to celebrate my aunt's wedding.

Then I saw my uncle Aiden and Mom walking down the aisle after me and Alex.

"Why do they look like the perfect couple?" I thought. Mom was smiling, and Uncle Aiden was holding her hand so passionately. "You can clearly see that connection," I said to myself.

As we waited for the rest to reach the front of the church, we saw my dad beginning to walk down the aisle with Aunt Kelani, who was tearing up. Zander locked eyes on her, and then his tears flowed. I noticed they were both crying.

"A true match made in Heaven," I said, trying not to cry also.

The ceremony began, and I listened as the minister spoke, thinking about me and Alex one day.

"Dearly beloved," the minister began, and the church fell quiet.

As the ceremony continued, I glanced over, and Alex was blowing kisses at me.

"I now pronounce you man and wife," the minister said. "Now you may kiss your bride."

Zander gave Aunt Kelani a long, passionate kiss.

Afterwards, we started taking some pictures inside the church and then moved outside. The photographer captured a shot of Zander and

Kelani just as the sun was about to set.

"It's simply breathtaking," I told Alex.

"I know it will turn out great," Alex said. "Look at the colors in the sky—so bright."

As we made our way to the reception, I noticed Uncle Aiden received a call.

"Let Henry and Stan handle that," Uncle Aiden replied. "We're at a wedding and not to be disturbed today."

Hours later, while we were all dancing and enjoying ourselves, Henry texted Uncle Aiden again. The message must have been devastating because I noticed my uncle's body language change instantly.

Then the DJ told us to join the newly married couple on the dance floor. Daddy told Uncle Aiden to dance with Mommy, and I was shocked. Anyone watching them could see the strong bond between them. "They can't deny it," I whispered to Alex. "Everyone sees it—except my Dad. Or does he?"

Zander told Kelani that she had made him the happiest man in the world. Kelani cried and replied,

"Zander, I have a surprise for you."

Zander looked puzzled. "What is it, my love?"

"Well, you know we're having twins—but we're having a boy and a girl," Kelani said.

Zander kissed her. "That's why I love you."

Then Aunt Kelani threw her wedding bouquet—and guess who caught it? I did. "I hope Alex catches the garter," I whispered to myself.

Zander threw the garter, and Alex did catch it—then placed it on my thigh.

As the newlyweds were about to leave, Alex and I decided to put "Just Married" on the back window of Zander's SUV. The rest of the wedding party threw rice at Uncle Zander and Aunt Kelani as they left the reception, blowing kisses before driving off.

Zander's assistant packed up the wedding gifts and took them to the house while the newlyweds went on their honeymoon—unknown to us.

Everyone was happy that Aunt Kelani's older kids and grandbabies showed up, making the day even more special for her as well as Zander. The photographer caught some pictures of them all together and showed them to Grandma Ida and Mommy.

"I can't wait to see all the pictures," Grandma Ida said.

Later, Daddy and Uncle Aiden started talking. Uncle Aiden read the last message sent to Daddy, and we overheard Daddy tell Mr. Stan to make sure Zander and Kelani had extra security on their honeymoon.

Back at the hotel later that night, I noticed a piece of paper on the desk in my parents' room. Looking closer, I saw it was a picture of me and Alex lying on the black sand, enjoying the beach.

"Oh my God—was Shane there, watching us?" I thought in shock.

I went into my room and started feeling really anxious.

"Jayla, are you alright?" Alex asked after noticing me nervously pacing.
"Come join me outside on the balcony," Alex said. "It's an amazing night—let's enjoy it together."

After changing my clothes, I joined Alex on the balcony, watching the Las Vegas lights. Alex held me close, making me feel safe.

"One day, you and I will be sharing our own wedding day just like this—with our loved ones watching us tie the knot," Alex whispered in my ear.

We talked about the kind of wedding we would have. Alex asked where I would like to get married. I told him Tahiti was nice, or maybe Italy, or some other destination. Then he asked what wedding color theme we might choose.

"Maybe navy blue or silver," Alex suggested. "And maybe you could have an unusual gown—not so traditional."

I thought about it and said maybe a pink or pastel color, but then I changed my mind. "Maybe something bright like orange, red, or yellow." Alex smiled. "No matter what color you choose, you'll be a beautiful bride—just like your Aunt Kelani was today."

"I can't wait to marry you," I told him, "to walk down the aisle to greet you. You'll make such a handsome groom."

Alex turned me around to face him. "When that day comes, I'll be just as happy—if not happier—than Zander was today."

"Well, prepare to see me crying more than my aunt," I teased. "I'll be a mess walking down the aisle."

We shared a kiss as the Vegas lights sparkled brightly behind us. Then I sat on Alex's lap, watching the nightlife from our balcony, lost in thoughts of our future together.

Chapter 8:
I Don't Want to Say Goodbye; We Just Said Hello

We had just gotten back from Vegas a few days ago, and I felt sicker now than I did before we left. *Could I really be pregnant?* I wondered.

I couldn't get over how beautiful my Aunt Kelani looked on her wedding day. I was so happy for them both, truly. And I loved being near the whole family. I wished nothing but happiness for Uncle Zander and Aunt Kelani—they both deserved it, and each other.

Maybe I would turn in early. Besides, I had to go back to work, and I was really tired—so that wasn't a bad idea.

"Guess we'll see each other after work," Alex said. "Love you, Blue Jay.

Hope you feel better."

"Night, Alex. I hope so too," I replied.

"I honestly do love you, Jayla," Alex told me, then kissed my forehead and left for his room.

The next morning, I woke up feeling terrible. *I think it's time to go to the doctor's for a check-up,* I told myself. *I've been so sick and tired since we got back from Tahiti, not even knowing why.*

"Good morning, Blue Jay. Where are you headed?" Mommy asked.

"I'm going to see Dr. Jazmine and get checked out," I told her.

"Oh, good to hear. I'm on my way out also," Mommy replied.

"Really? Where?" I asked.

"To also see Dr. Jazmine," she said.

I was shocked. "When is your appointment, Mommy?"

"In an hour," I replied. "Why, when is yours?"

"Before yours, clearly," Mommy answered, sipping juice.

"Let's go together to Dr. Jazmine's office," I suggested.

We didn't say anything in the car ride over, just stayed quiet until we entered the office. First, Mommy had her appointment, and when she came out, she looked shocked.

"Ma, Mommy, you alright? Talk to me," I asked. "Well, tell me."

"I'm... I'm... well, I found out that I'm... pregnant," Mommy said.

She froze, her hand covering her mouth, as though the memory of *when* it happened hit her all at once back in Tahiti.

"Daddy will be totally shocked at this," I said quietly.

Mommy looked down and whispered, "It's not your Daddy's baby, Blue Jay." Silent tears rolled down her cheeks.

I hugged her tightly. That's when I understood, the baby Mommy was carrying was Uncle Aiden's.

"Please don't say anything to your Dad until I figure out what to do," Mom said, her voice dazed, still in shock.

"I love you, Mommy, and I'm not going to judge you," I replied. "Because the heart wants what the heart wants," I told her.

The nurse then called me to follow her into the room where Mom had just left. "Mommy tells me, 'Blue Jay, I am going to be right here waiting for you.'" I smiled nervously. "Please follow me," the nurse said.

A few minutes later, the door opened, but I came out crying. "Blue Jay, baby, talk to me, sweetheart," Mommy said.

"Mom, Mommy, don't be mad, but I'm knocked up," I told her.

"Oh, Blue Jay, I'm not mad. But how do you feel about that news?" Mommy asked me.

"It had to be when Alex and I had sex during the Christmas holiday, when Alex got me pregnant," I said. "We were having sex a lot during the Christmas vacation."

"How is this going to look?" I thought. "Both mother and daughter are pregnant at the same time?"

"You don't worry about what others say or think," Mom said. "Me and your Dad will be there for you, and you already know Alex will."

"Ahh, my baby is having a baby," Mom said in a happy, tearful voice.

"Daddy is going to flip or have a cow when he finds out," I said.

"Not to worry, I will be with you when you tell him," Mom said. "Your Dad will be fine; besides, he knows you are not a little girl anymore, but you are a young woman."

"We will be there with you every step of the way," Mommy assured me. "What about you, Mommy?" I asked.

"What about me?" she said. "Who will be there for you?" I asked.

"Jayla, Mommy and Uncle Aiden made this bed, and we will have to lie in it," Mommy said, being brave.

"No matter what, as your parents, we'll be there for you and Alex," Mommy assured me again. "No matter what happens with her and my Dad, it won't change how they love me."

"Come, Blue Jay, let's go get us something to eat," Mommy suggested. "Any suggestions?" she asked.

"No, not really hungry right now, Mommy," I said.

"Hate to tell you, Jayla, but you have to eat because you are expecting," Mommy told me.

"We can then go to the bookstore and get you some books to read,"

Mommy suggested. "But hands-on is going to be your best teacher," she said jokingly.

"I love you so much, my Jayla; your heart is big like mine," Mommy said. "I can't believe I'm about to be a grandma, auntie, oh, and mom," she thought.

"I am going to be a big sister, big cousin, and a mom," I replied.

"Mommy, I have your back when you decide to tell Dad about what happened in Tahiti with Uncle Aiden," I replied.

"Oh my God, I have to text Alex and let him know," I thought.

"Are you really going to tell Alex in a text?" Mommy asked me.

"Yes, fine. I will tell Alex to text me as soon as he reads the message; that's better," I replied.

"Mommy, can I ask you about what's happening with you and Uncle Aiden?" I asked. "Or is it not my business?" I added.

"How are you feeling now, Jayla?" Mommy asked.

"I don't feel as sick once we ate," I replied.

"These prenatal pills should help you also," Mommy said. "I will tell Ms. Gracie to make sure you get a snack at night from now on," Mommy added.

"We can do our appointments together if you want to," Mommy suggested. I agreed it would be a great idea.

"Start reading these books to get some insight," Mom suggested.

"So, Jayla, have you thought about when you are going to tell your Dad the news?" Mom hinted.

"Tonight at dinner," I told Mom. "Just to get it over with," I said. "I pray my Dad doesn't decide to put Alex out."

"I would leave with Alex for real, Mommy, because I love Alex," I told her.

"Listen, Blue Jay, your Dad is a lot of things, but family is always family, no matter what," Mom said. "Besides, if your Dad ever thought about putting you out, he would have to deal with me."

"Thank you again, Stan," Mommy said. "Will you please take the bags to Jayla's room?" Mommy asked him.

"Ms. Gracie, can you tell Giovanni that me and Jayla are back home?" Mommy requested.

"Yes, Ms. Katiana," Ms. Gracie replied. "May I fix you a drink first?" Ms. Gracie asked.

"Not right now," Mom replied. "But you can tell Jayla when she comes out of the bathroom to meet us in the living room," Katiana instructed.

"As you wish, Ms. Katiana. I will tell Ms. Jayla," Gracie replied.

"Oh, is Aiden here?" Katiana asked, trying not to sound pressed.

"Mr. Aiden has been in his room since he got back," Ms. Gracie replied.

"Shall I go get Mr. Aiden from his room for you?" Ms. Gracie asked Katiana.

"No," she replied. "But can you tell him Katiana would like to talk to him later in private?" Katiana told Ms. Gracie.

"Why hasn't Alex texted me back yet?" I wondered. "Alex should have been home by now," I thought as I looked out my window for his car.

"That still sounds weird, saying 'home, '" I thought.

"Daddy, oh Daddy, hey, have you seen Alex?" I asked.

"Hello, my Blue Jay, and how are you feeling?" Daddy asked.

61

"I've been better, Daddy, believe me," I replied under my breath.

"What's wrong, Blue Jay? Are you coming down with something?" Daddy asked me.

"Daddy, answer me, have you seen Alex?" I asked again. "Alex isn't here yet," Daddy replied, looking puzzled.

"Alex should have been here by now; he left work a few minutes before I did," Daddy replied. "I assumed Alex had already arrived a few minutes ahead of me," Daddy said.

"Have you tried calling him?" Mommy asked, trying not to make me panic.

"I will try to call Alex's phone again," I said. "Excuse me for a minute, please. But when I come back, can we talk, Daddy?" I asked.

"Katiana, are you feeling better now?" Daddy asked Mommy as I was leaving the room.

"Giovanni, can we talk when we finish with Blue Jay?" Katiana asked.

"Of course, it sounds important. Anything wrong?" Giovanni replied.

"Katiana, no matter what, I will always love you," Giovanni told her.

"Pardon me, Vanni, may I have a word with you in private?" Stan asked.

"This sounds serious. What's wrong?" Giovanni asked Stan.

"It's very serious, and you need to leave quickly. It's about Mr. Alex," Stan said.

"Tell me, Stan, what's so important that needs my attention?" Giovanni asked.

"Alex has been in a terrible accident and is being flown to the hospital as we speak," Stan replied to Giovanni.

"Get the car ready," Giovanni told Stan as Aiden walked down the hall. "Aiden, Aiden, come here," Giovanni called out. "What's wrong, Giovanni?" Aiden asked him.

"Alex has been in a terrible accident and has been seriously hurt," Stan told Giovanni.

"Daddy, did I hear you right? Alex has been in a terrible accident?" I asked in the doorway, shocked.

"Yes, Blue Jay, you heard me right, and we're on our way to the hospital," Giovanni replied.

"Oh my God, Daddy!" I just started screaming. Uncle Aiden held onto me.

"Alex, you can't die, Alex, you can't die now," I kept repeating over and over.

"Don't think negatively, Jayla baby, think positively," Mommy told me.

"Let's go, Blue Jay, let's go into the hospital and get some information," Mommy said, holding my hand.

"Excuse me, excuse me, can you help me, please?" I asked the woman at the desk.

"I am trying to find out about my boyfriend, Alex Jensen. He has been in an accident, and I need some answers," I said.

"Are you his next of kin or a family member?" the hospital staff member asked me.

"Yes, we are," Daddy replied, now pushing me aside and taking over.

"And who are you, sir, to Mr. Jensen?" the staff member asked Daddy.

"I'm Mr. Jensen's Father-in-Law, Giovanni Harrison," Daddy replied.

"One moment," she replied, and said that the doctor would speak to us before we're let into his room, the staff member said.

"Put this ring on quickly," Daddy told me. "Remember, you are married to Alex, got that?" Daddy said under his breath, before the lady came back.

"Mr. Harrison, nice to meet you. I'm Dr. Kerrs. I'm the one taking care of your Son-in-Law, Alex Jensen," the doctor replied.

"Can you please tell us what exactly happened to my Son-in-Law?" Giovanni asked Dr. Kerrs.

I suddenly felt like I was underwater, and then I heard that Alex lost control of his vehicle and someone called it in. We have no more information at this time, Dr. Kerrs told Daddy. Uncle Aiden saw me getting dizzy and caught me. "Jayla, Jayla baby, I got you," Uncle Aiden told me.

"How about we give your daughter a sedative to relax?" Dr. Kerrs suggested.

"Will it hurt my baby? It can't hurt the baby," I asked him.

Daddy overheard me and turned towards me. "Jayla, did you just ask if it will harm the baby?"

"I was going to tell you at dinner that I was pregnant, Daddy," I said.

Daddy kissed me and expressed how excited he was. "Really, Daddy?" I asked him, just surprised by his reaction.

"I love Alex as if he were my own son," Dad said. "I'm just glad to see you happy, and clearly you are with Alex," Dad said.

Uncle Aiden hugged me, also happy, and kissed my forehead, then got me a ginger ale.

Then, a few minutes later, I went in to finally see Alex. Dear God, Alex had so many tubes - one in his mouth, one in his chest, one in his stomach, I noticed. Alex's face was so swollen and bruised from hitting the steering wheel.

I leaned down and kissed Alex and whispered in his ear. "Alex, you're going to be a daddy. Alex, we are pregnant," I said.

"I just found out today, so Alex, you have to get better because we need you," I told him.

Then, all of a sudden, an alarm went off on Alex's bed. "Oh no, what's happening to him?" I asked as the doctors came running into his room. "Is Alex going to be okay?" I started yelling as I watched them work on Alex.

"We need a crash cart," one of the nurses suddenly yelled.

"Code Blue room ICU#25," another nurse called overhead.

"Mommy, Mommy, what's happening to Alex?" I asked, crying.

"Blue Jay, let them do their job, baby," Mom replied. "Come over here with me," Mommy told me.

A few minutes later, Dr. Kerrs called Daddy over and told him something. Daddy then got a puzzled look on his face. I knew then that it wasn't good news about Alex. I sighed.

"Alex had internal bleeding along with several broken ribs, and a punctured lung," Dr. Kerrs told Daddy.

"I have to call Kirk and let him know about Alex and bring him here," Dad said.

"I already called him," Uncle Aiden told Daddy. "The plane is going to pick him and Dayonna up."

"Thank you so much, Uncle Aiden," I said, hardly able to speak from crying.

"Excuse me, I have to take this call," Uncle Aiden said and walked away.

"Jayla, how are you holding up, baby girl? We're still praying," Mom replied.

"Daddy seemed excited about the baby news," I replied to Mommy.

"I told you your Daddy is not so scary," Mom said with a half-smile.

"Do you want to sit down and rest your legs?" Mommy asked. "And before you say no, think about the baby inside you," Mommy replied.

"You can lay your head on Mommy's lap, Blue Jay," she said.

I dozed off and then woke right back up a few minutes later. When I couldn't keep still, I walked back into Alex's room and lay my head on his chest to hear his heartbeat.

All I could do was pray that Alex makes it and we raise our child together, then get married.

"Alex, can you hear me?" I asked. "If you can hear me, Alex baby, please open your eyes," I replied.

"So I can see your sexy eyes one more time if you die," I said.

Alex's eyes began to blink rapidly, as if he was trying to see me one last time.

"If you can hear me, blink once," I said to see what Alex would do.

He blinked. I nearly screamed. "Alex, you blinked! I saw you!"

"Hey, Mom, Dad, Alex just blinked for me. Come watch! Watch, are you watching?" I replied, then asked Alex again.

"Alex, baby, if you can hear me, blink once again to show Mommy and Daddy?"

"Look, you see that, Mommy? Daddy, did you see that?" I said, smiling.

"Nurse, Nurse, please come quickly," Mommy told her. "Look, I told the Nurse now to show her, so I said it again."

"If you can hear me, Alex, please open your eyes, for the Nurse to see?"

And just then, Alex's eyes began to rapidly flicker, like he was trying to open them.

It was now 3:30, and Uncle Aiden came around the corner with some drinks and something to eat. Daddy had Alex put on his very own separate floor so that we could have it all to ourselves to sleep in peace or just to simply not be bothered.

"Have Kirk and Dayonna arrived yet?" I asked.

"They should be here in two hours," Uncle Aiden replied.

"Stan, what else did you find out about Alex's accident?" Uncle Aiden asked him.

Uncle Aiden suddenly punched the wall, and Mommy and I just looked his way, trying to understand why he did it.

Then Mommy walked down there to see what was wrong with Uncle Aiden.

"Your Mom is the only woman that can calm down your Uncle Aiden," Daddy replied.

"Aiden, please let the nurse look at your hand to see if you broke something," Mommy suggested to him.

"That motherfucker is going to pay when I find him," Aiden told Katiana.

Daddy then walked down there to see why Aiden was pissed. "Aiden, tell me what's got you so pissed, what did Stan tell you about the accident?"

"Vanni, Stan just told me that he hasn't found out anything," Aiden said before Giovanni replied, "Aiden, before you lie to me, make sure the story is believable. I can see you are really furious, Aiden, about Stan's finding. Don't forget Stan is great at his job, just as you are."

"I will check on Jayla and let you men talk," Mommy replied and walked back up the hallway towards me.

Aiden then told Giovanni that Arturo was caught leaving Alex's crash after it happened.

"So you think Arturo had something to do with Alex's accident?" Giovanni asked Aiden.

"Strong possibility," Aiden replied. "And so does Stan. Stan has got our best men checking and trying to find out stuff along with Henry," Aiden replied.

"Our mechanic looked over Alex's car and said he noticed his brake line was cut."

The next thing I heard was a familiar voice as I was waking up from my nap. Dayonna and Kirk were quickly coming down the hallway.

I got up and hugged Kirk and then hugged Dayonna, who has always been my rock.

Dayonna asked me if we could talk; it was something she wanted to share.

"Dayonna tells me that she had some news to share with me?"

"I have some news to share with you," I said quietly. "Dayonna, you first—what's your news?"

"I'm pregnant, Jayla," Dayonna told me.

I froze, stunned.

"Dayonna... I'm also pregnant," I admitted, my voice trembling. "I just found out today."

Dayonna's eyes widened, then she hugged me tight.

"I was going to tell Alex my news after he got off work," I whispered, tears starting to spill, "but instead we're here..."

"Calm down, Jayla," Dayonna said gently. "Do you know what happened?"

"All I know is that Alex was in some type of accident on his way home," I managed to say.

Then it hit me—I had texted Alex earlier. My stomach twisted.

"Oh no, Dayonna... what if my text made him swerve?" My voice cracked. "Maybe that one text caused Alex's accident."

"Jayla, stop. You had nothing to do with Alex's accident," Uncle Aiden said firmly.

"How do you know for sure, Uncle Aiden?" I asked, desperate.

Uncle Aiden's face hardened. "Because Alex's brake line had been cut."

I gasped, my hands flying to my mouth.

"Where did Kirk go?" Dayonna asked him.

"He went in there to see Alex," I said. "Do you want me to show you his room?"

"Your Dad is in there with Kirk," I added softly. "I guess Dr. Kerrs is telling him what he told us about Alex's prognosis."

"I can't believe we're both pregnant," I murmured, still dazed.

Dayonna sniffled. "How did your mom take the news about you being knocked up?"

"Not well," she admitted. "So me and Kirk moved into your old house. My mom was livid." Tears glistened in her eyes.

"Give your mom some time—or I can talk to her," Mommy suggested.

"Would you do that for me, Ms. Katiana?" Dayonna asked hopefully.

"Of course," Mommy nodded.

"Thank you, Ms. Katiana. I'd really appreciate that," Dayonna said softly.

"You girls want something to eat?" Uncle Aiden asked. "I was about to order some food here."

"You girls need to eat—even if it's just a piece of fruit," Mommy reminded us.

A few days passed, and we were on our way to see Alex. But as soon as we stepped into the hallway, we saw doctors and nurses rushing toward his room.

"Code blue, code blue, room twenty-five!" a nurse shouted.

My heart plummeted. Mommy grabbed me before my knees buckled, while Dayonna clutched Kirk. Dad tried to push into the room, but they held him back.

Moments later, Dad returned to the waiting room where we all sat, tense and silent, as Dr. Kerrs walked in. His face was grave.

"I'm so sorry," he began, and before he even finished, my tears fell.

"Mr. Jensen had a massive attack... and he didn't make it."

A scream tore from my throat. My parents and Uncle Aiden held onto me as if I might collapse. Dayonna and Kirk broke down too, clinging to each other.

"No, no—Alex, you can't be gone!" I sobbed, the words spilling out again and again as the world around me blurred.

Dr. Kerrs explained to Uncle Aiden that Alex had suffered severe internal bleeding—his body filling with blood until, in the end, he had suffocated in it. The words hit like a hammer, leaving me numb.

Daddy spoke quietly to the social worker, telling her that whatever belongings Alex had from the accident, we would take home with us. My eyes caught on a small velvet box among the items. My chest tightened. A ring box.

Oh no... Alex was going to propose to me tonight.

Tears blurred my vision as I remembered—Alex had already asked both Uncle Aiden and Daddy for my hand when we were in Tahiti. He had been planning this.

When we finally returned to the house, I slipped away to the guest house, needing to be near him somehow. Inside the front room, the walls were lined with pictures—our Christmas vacation smiles frozen in time, snapshots of all four of us back at the hotel when we first met.

The sight undid me. I collapsed onto the couch, sobbing uncontrollably.

"Alex... I can't believe you're gone. You won't even get to see our son or daughter born." My voice cracked, rising into a raw scream. "Why did you have to leave me now?"

The door creaked open, and Uncle Aiden stepped in. I stumbled into his arms, burying my face against his chest as sobs wracked me. He just held me, silent and steady, not realizing that Mom was watching us quietly from the doorway. And in that moment, Mom knew what she had to do.

That night, I lay in bed staring at the ceiling, sleepless. Downstairs, Mommy and Grandma Ida worked on Alex's funeral arrangements. Mommy had already called Aunt Kelani and Uncle Zander to tell them the heartbreaking news—and to share some other news as well.

In the morning, I walked downstairs to find Grandma Ida waiting. She wrapped me in a warm, firm hug.

"My condolences, baby," she whispered. "Alex was like part of this family."

Her words cracked something inside me, but then she pulled back and smiled softly.

"Oh, I hear congratulations are in order too."

I shook my head. "I don't feel like it's a blessing anymore."

Grandma's hand smoothed over my tummy. "He or she is a blessing, Jayla. You still have a part of Alex with you, even though he's gone."

Tears welled up again. "I don't know what to do, Grandma."

"We've got your back, baby. That's what family is for. And we'll be here for Dayonna and Kirk too—they're part of this family as much as you are."

"Where are they, anyway?" Grandma asked.

"They left a few hours ago. They're thinking about moving closer to me," I told her.

Daddy, listening nearby, spoke up. "We can fix up the old garage house for them—with some upgrades, of course. It would be attached to the guest house."

Uncle Aiden nodded. "That way you'd still feel close to Alex."

"You're right, Dad," I said softly. "I do feel closer to him down there."

"No, that wasn't me," Daddy corrected gently. "It was your uncle Aiden and your mommy who thought of it. I'm just making sure the upgrades happen—alongside your uncle."

I gave him a watery smile. "That still counts as something, Daddy. Thank you. And thank you for covering the extra costs, too."

"No problem, Blue Jay. Alex was—and will forever be—family," Daddy said firmly.

Gratitude swelled in my chest. I'm so lucky to have such a loving family.

Just then, Grandpa Vince walked in. I rushed to hug him tightly.

"Hey, Blue Jay," he said, his voice rough with sympathy. "My condolences about poor Alex. I liked him. Strong handshake, that one."

He pulled back, eyes twinkling with a smile meant to cheer me. "I hope you have a boy, Blue Jay—so he can throw balls with his great-grandpa."

Grandma Diva, never one to be left out, chimed in with a playful grin. "Jay Bird, I hope you have a girl, so she can go shopping with her great-grandma."

I sat outside in the garden, the air heavy with silence, trying to make sense of Alex's death. Pregnant, alone, and aching, I kept asking myself—what is my next move?

Through the open window, I overheard Uncle Aiden talking quietly to Daddy.

"Stan came across footage of Alex's crash," he said, his voice low. "There was a figure in a hoodie. Looked like he was talking to Alex...

maybe even leaning in toward him. Hard to say."

"Then you see the ambulance pulling up, but whoever it is never shows their face," Uncle Aiden added.

My chest tightened. "I want to see the tape," I told them both, stepping into the room.

But Daddy and Uncle Aiden exchanged a look.

"Blue Jay," Daddy said gently, "in your condition, it's better you don't."

"You need to think about the baby," Uncle Aiden added.

I wanted to argue, but the tears came first. I ran back to my room, collapsed onto the bed, and cried. Deep down, I knew they were right—but the not-knowing gnawed at me.

The following week, Aunt Kelani and Uncle Zander came to pay their respects and to stand with us in celebrating Alex's homecoming. Mommy and Grandma Ida had poured their hearts into the funeral arrangements.

"It was our pleasure, Blue Jay," Mommy said softly. "Alex deserved it."

Inside the church, the sight stopped me cold. Part of Alex's face was visible above the open casket—a polished chrome one with his name engraved along the side. Resting beside him was a framed photo of the two of us and the sonogram of our baby.

A sob caught in my throat, and my legs gave way. Uncle Aiden grabbed my arm before I could fall, guiding me to a pew. "Sit, breathe," he whispered, pressing a bottled water into my hand. I kissed his cheek with trembling lips, then wiped at my wet eyes.

Mommy and Grandma Ida moved gracefully through the gathering, greeting Alex's family and friends—faces I barely remembered, people who had grown up with him and Kirk. Their voices and handshakes blurred together for me.

When the service began, my parents sat on one side, Uncle Aiden on the other, and Dayonna and Kirk just beyond him. The priest's voice carried over Alex, but my mind kept drifting. I couldn't take it all in—my heart wasn't ready to let him go.

I kept staring at Alex lying there in his navy blue suit, the same way I had pictured him dressed on our wedding day. Handsome. Still. Too still.

Then the funeral assistant stepped forward.

"If anyone would like to come up one last time to say goodbye, please do so now."

The words rang like a bell in my ears. My body wouldn't move. My legs felt bolted to the floor.

Uncle Aiden leaned close, his hand warm on my arm. Without a word, he helped me rise, steadying me as we walked together toward the casket.

I leaned down and pressed a long kiss against Alex's cold, hard lips. The finality of it broke me, and I collapsed back into Uncle Aiden's arms. He guided me gently to my seat.

As the funeral assistants began closing the casket lid, I shook my head in disbelief. My sobs tore through the quiet church. Watching the lid descend felt like watching the world close in on me—I wanted to scream for them to stop, to give me just one more second.

"This concludes the services for Alex Collin Jensen," the priest announced solemnly. "You are welcome to join the family at the Luminaria Restaurant and Patio for the repast."

Later, we drove to Alex's favorite place—our beach. He once told me it was where he found peace, where the sunsets felt like promises. Now, it was where we laid him to rest. His chrome casket glistened in the sun as they lowered it into the ground, inch by inch, until it disappeared from sight. My cries grew raw, my voice breaking.

"Jayla, baby, let's go," Mommy whispered, tugging gently at my arm.

"Mommy, I can't leave Alex alone," I sobbed.

"Alex is not alone," she replied, trying to steer me toward the car.

"I can't do this! I want Alex back!" I cried, clinging to her as she simply held me tighter.

At the restaurant afterward, I finally told the family I was pregnant. Gasps filled the room, but Aunt Kelani only smiled softly, her eyes shining with understanding. I barely touched my food. When we returned home, I slipped straight into the guest house, needing to feel close to Alex. I replayed our last videos together, the sound of his laugh piercing through my tears.

A knock on the door pulled me from my grief. "Jayla, can I come in?" Mommy asked. She stepped inside and wrapped me in her arms.

"You alright, baby?" she murmured.

"No," I whispered into her shoulder.

"Your father and uncle want you to see something," she said gently.

In the office, Daddy motioned toward the screen. "Jayla, I need you to look at this. Tell me if this person looks familiar."

I sat down, my hands trembling as the footage of Alex's accident played. Tears streamed down my face. Uncle Aiden slid his hand into mine. And then I saw it—the shadowed figure in a hoodie leaning toward Alex's car.

My breath caught. "That's him!" I screamed. "That's Shane!"

Daddy's jaw tightened, and he exchanged a furious look with Uncle Aiden.

"Look closer," Uncle Aiden urged. "He's... he's reading Alex's phone." His voice cracked in shock.

Horror twisted in my stomach. Oh God—Shane knows I'm pregnant. My chest heaved. If Shane knew... what would he do to me now?

"At least he called for help," I whispered brokenly. "But it still didn't save Alex."

"I'm sorry you had to see that," Uncle Aiden said softly. "It couldn't have been easy."

I pushed back from the desk, my voice shaky. "I have to go now, Daddy."

"Pumpkin, I'll check on you later," Daddy called after me as I walked out, tears still stinging my eyes.

Back at the guest house—now connected to the main house so I could eat with the family or slip to the pool—I shut the door behind me. But no walls could keep out the fear curling in my chest.

Chapter 9:
Secrets Are Revealed from the Past

A few days later, I went to the spa to get a massage to help me relax and get used to the new normal without Alex being here with me.

I stopped by the doctor's because I was having some anxiety, and she prescribed some medicine that wouldn't harm the baby.

I started to relax and then heard the door opening. I asked for a cold drink of juice.

When I got my juice, a few minutes later I started feeling dizzy. Then I noticed a figure at the door with a hoodie, and then it went dark.

I started to open my eyes and noticed Arturo had me in some sort of warehouse.

"What do you want with me?" I asked. "Should I call you Shane or Arturo?"

"Arturo will be fine," he replied. "And should I offer my congratulations on your new addition?" Then he rubbed my belly. I pushed his hand away.

"How did you know I was pregnant?" I asked Arturo.

"I saw it in a text once," Arturo replied very sarcastically.

"I knew it was you on that tape," I replied, crying, thinking about Alex.

"Guilty as charged," Arturo said.

I just shook my head, getting pissed.

"Jayla, my sweetness, why do you look so sad?" Arturo replied.

"Don't call me that," I replied.

"By the way, my real name is Arturo, not Shane, as you already know.

I started messing with you to get revenge on your dad for firing me," he told me. "Then I fell in love with you, Jayla," he said. "And I started to really enjoy making you moan my name. I know I wasn't supposed to fall in love with you," he said.

"You are one sick bastard," I told Arturo.

"You killed your ex-girlfriend and her parents," I said.

"Because they pissed me off," Arturo told me.

"How could you do that to someone you loved?" I asked him.

"Because they were going to tell the cops and they blackmailed me," Arturo replied. "So I had to get rid of them," he replied, looking evil.

"Do you know how it hurt me watching you and Alex make love?" Arturo asked me.

"I just wanted to kill him after the first time Alex fucked you," Arturo said.

"You've been following me and Alex?" I asked Arturo.

"I had to make sure you were safe, babe," Arturo replied, feeling my hair.

"Don't touch me, you sick fuck," I told Arturo.

"Oh, and to answer your question, Jayla. I am the reason that made dear Alex run off the road," Arturo told me.

"I cut Alex's brake line while he was at work." My heart dropped just hearing that.

"Then I wanted to see the guy up close who stole my baby away from me," Arturo replied.

I was speechless.

"Then I saw that new message that you sent him," Arturo said. "And then I read the message to Alex that you were pregnant and that you loved him instead of me," Arturo said in a mad voice.

"So as Alex started losing consciousness, I reminded dear Alex that you were always going to be my girl. And all Alex kept saying was that he loved you. And that's when I just saw red," Arturo replied.

That's when I knew Arturo did what he did to Alex.

"But I called 911 because of my love for you, Jayla," Arturo told me.

"Don't touch me, you murderer!" I screamed at Arturo.

"I have to admit it was hard following you two around town without your family catching me," Arturo said, half laughing.

"Aiden's men are very good at their job," Arturo replied. "I should know because I used to be one of them," Arturo replied.

"I have had so many fantasies about making love to you ever since I saw you undressing in your room," Arturo said.

"You were watching me sleeping?" I asked Arturo.

"I thought I was caught when you came to the window, but good ole Mr. Stan gave me a way out," Arturo smirked.

"It was you at my window?" I asked Arturo. "It was you that made that noise, wasn't it?"

"Had I been able to get in your room, Jayla, I would have fucked your brains out for old times' sake," Arturo replied. "But I know why Alex enjoyed fucking you just as much as I did," Arturo replied, touching my leg.

"Oh, my dear Jayla, you have no idea how much I missed you," Arturo said.

I also saw you and Alex making love in Tahiti," Arturo said. "And let me say this—you made me play with myself that night," Arturo replied.

"Watching you two making love in the sand reminded me of us back in the day when you were my girl," Arturo said.

"Well, I'm not your girl anymore and never will be," I told him.

"But you can be my girl again," Arturo replied. "Alex and Alissa are gone. I can help you take care of the baby, and we can be a family," Arturo told me.

"You need help, Arturo. You're sick," I told him.

"Tahiti was also very exciting for your mom and Uncle Aiden as well," Arturo replied next.

"Oh no—he saw my mom," I said to myself.

"I watched them two make love on the beach as well," Arturo told me. "Your mom definitely got pregnant that night," Arturo said, laughing. "Your uncle Aiden—or should I say your father—really fucked your mom that night," Arturo replied.

"What are you talking about now, Arturo?"

"They never told you, did they, Jayla?" Arturo told me.

"Tell me what?" I asked Arturo, looking puzzled.

"Then please let me enlighten you about something," Arturo replied. "When you were born, Giovanni wanted to know if he was your uncle or father. Giovanni felt that your mom was already pregnant with you before they made love—by your uncle Aiden. Well, shall I say by your biological father," Arturo said sarcastically.

"You see, Giovanni can't have kids due to an accident he had when he was little," Arturo told me.

"You're lying, Arturo. Stop lying to me," I told him.

"Am I lying to you, Jayla? Here, look at these." Arturo handed me some papers. "Look for yourself," Arturo said. "Here are all the documents," Arturo replied.

"I was Giovanni's main man and knew about family secrets before he fired me," Arturo said.

"So you believe me now?" Arturo asked me. But I was still reading the papers.

"So when you all went to Vegas for your Aunt Kelani's wedding—by the way, she looked amazing—I noticed your mom going in his room and leaving Aiden a message," Arturo said. "But your mommy didn't realize she dropped it in the hallway," Arturo smirked.

"So I had to make sure Daddy read it and let him know what your mom and Aiden were up to in Tahiti," Arturo said.

"Giovanni didn't get mad, which pissed me off," Arturo said. "Giovanni told me he knew they had always had that type of chemistry between themselves. But when I sent Giovanni those pictures of Aiden fucking your mom in the sand..." Arturo smiled. "Oh, Giovanni got so heated, and it made me proud," Arturo replied.

"Giovanni stayed out all night, but Aiden—I'm sure he fucked your mom good that night in the hotel," Arturo said.

"I have to admit, me and Giovanni were the best of friends. But Aiden—oh, how I hate him. We really never saw eye to eye after that accident. Aiden made sure he told Giovanni what he suspected me of doing, and then I got fired."

"Why did you have to kill Alex?" I asked Arturo, tearing up.

"Alex had to die, Jayla, because every time I saw you two kissing or saw Alex fucking you, I heard you moaning his name," Arturo said. "So Alex had to go. Alex was touching you, and it made me crazy," Arturo said.

"All I saw was you and Alex fucking when I closed my eyes," Arturo replied. "And you're mine, Jayla."

"I hate you so much right now, Arturo. You broke my heart," I told him.

"You got mad at me because I didn't see you anymore," I told Arturo.

"Alex did nothing to you," I told Arturo. "Your frustration and hate were for me."

Meanwhile, back at the house, Mommy had asked Ms. Gracie if I had come back from the spa yet. Katiana checked the guest house and then called the spa. The receptionist told my mom they would check the room I was in.

"They say Jayla might have fallen asleep," the receptionist replied.

Aiden called Giovanni and told him to come take a look at the surveillance camera at the spa. Aiden explained that a buddy noticed something strange and contacted him quickly.

Aiden and Giovanni began looking, and all of a sudden they noticed a hooded man carrying someone out the back door.

"Oh my God," Giovanni said. "Is that my baby Jayla?"

Aiden rewound the tape and looked closely. "Arturo—it's Arturo," Aiden said, slamming his fist on the desk.

"What does Arturo want with my baby girl?" Giovanni asked.

"Arturo must know Jayla is pregnant and feels betrayed," Aiden thought aloud.

Then Giovanni and Aiden reported to Stan and considered some places Arturo might have taken me. Aiden asked Giovanni if he still had access to their old abandoned warehouses outside of town.

"Yes," Giovanni replied.

"Let's get some extra manpower. We need all the help we can get," Aiden said, then started making phone calls.

"Maybe include some cops," Giovanni suggested. "I don't want Arturo to go free on some sort of technicality."

"I'm going to kill Arturo if he hurts Jayla," Aiden told Giovanni.

"Aiden," Giovanni replied, "Arturo won't hurt Jayla. He's in love with her—in his own sick and twisted way."

"Arturo better not hurt my baby," Katiana said from the doorway.

"Katiana, we will bring our baby home safely," Aiden assured her.

Giovanni noticed Aiden hugging Katiana but stayed in the back, trying not to be noticed.

"Do you think Arturo caused Alex's accident?" Giovanni asked Aiden as they started driving toward the first of four warehouses.

"I have no doubt Arturo had a hand in killing Alex," Aiden replied. "Stan found out someone had cut Alex's brake line. Someone wanted to send us a message by doing that to Alex."

"And now Arturo has your baby girl and grandchild. We are going to bring them both back home safely," Aiden said, still driving.

"Please, God, keep them all safe," Katiana prayed.

"Ms. Katiana, what's going on? Where's Jayla—she's not answering her phone?"

"Come here and let me tell you what's happened," Katiana told Dayonna, then started explaining.

As Aiden and Giovanni headed toward the next warehouse, they told the cops to continue going in quietly, to sneak up on Arturo if he was inside. But another warehouse turned out empty, and they continued on to the next.

"Aiden," Giovanni said, "if something should happen, promise me you will take care of the family."

Aiden looked at Giovanni and replied, "You have my word. But I won't let anything happen to you. My word is my bond, and we will bring Blue Jay and the baby safely home—that's a promise."

Meanwhile, on the far side of town in the last warehouse, I asked Arturo, "Can you get me something to drink? I'm really thirsty—and maybe something to eat? I need to eat; being pregnant makes me nauseous sometimes."

"Arturo, are you listening to me?" I asked him.

"Shut up, Jayla. Please—I never realized how much you can talk," Arturo replied.

"If you ever loved me, could you find it in your heart to get me something to eat and drink?" I asked him.

Arturo left the room but then, a couple of minutes later, he handed me a ham and cheese sandwich and a bottle of cranberry grape juice.

"Thank you," I replied.

"Can you take these cuffs off? I need to use my hands to eat," I asked.

"Don't try anything stupid, Jayla, or you will be sorry," Arturo told me.

I began to eat while looking around to see if I could find a way to get away.

"Arturo, can I use the restroom? I have to pee," I asked him.

"You're asking for a lot, Jayla," Arturo replied.

"Really, I don't mean to, but I really need to go."

Arturo threw me a bucket. "Pee in that."

"You want me to pee in this nasty ass bucket?" I replied.

"It's either that nasty ass bucket or pee on yourself," Arturo said.

I began to pull my shorts down, but Arturo started to stare at me.

"Your belly has a little bump," Arturo said. "You look to be closer to two months than just a few weeks."

"Don't touch me, Arturo, or else—"

"Or else what?" Arturo asked, still touching me.

"No one will ever find you here," Arturo said, then grabbed me.

"Please, Arturo, no—you might hurt my baby," I said.

"Please don't do this." But it fell on deaf ears. Arturo pushed me onto the little mattress.

He began taking off my shorts and smelled my underwear. "You still smell delicious," Arturo said.

"You always smell so sweet," he added, smelling them again.

"Arturo—or Shane—please don't do this," I begged.

Arturo forced himself between my legs, and I tried pushing him off. Then he unzipped his pants and forced himself inside me. Arturo began thrusting hard and quickly.

"You're hurting me, Arturo, please stop—" He smacked my face hard, and I blacked out.

When I woke up, Arturo told me to be quiet because he thought he heard people talking outside.

I curled up, holding myself on the little cot where Arturo had raped me. A few minutes later, I noticed shadows.

Then I saw Uncle Aiden and Daddy sneaking up along the far wall.

"Welcome to the party," Arturo said. "We've been waiting for you."

"Let her go, Arturo," Giovanni told him. "You want me, not Jayla."

"No, I'm pretty sure Arturo wants me," Aiden said, walking toward him. "Because I made you fire him?"

"I hated you for that, Aiden," Arturo replied, cocking his gun.

"Blame yourself," Giovanni told Arturo. "You are the one who betrayed us."

"I had no choice," Arturo replied. "They were blackmailing me."

Stan and some other guys slowly surrounded Arturo.

"Hey, Aiden," Arturo sneered, "how does it feel to be the main man again?"

"Wonderful," Aiden replied. "I've always been the man. Now let Jayla go."

"Giovanni, tell me—how did it feel to know I was the one fucking your daughter, or should I say niece?" Arturo said. Giovanni looked puzzled.

"And Aiden, how does it feel to know you were really raising your daughter?" Aiden looked puzzled too.

"Giovanni, what is he talking about?" Aiden asked.

"Giovanni, do tell your brother how Katiana, your now-wife, was pregnant by him. And don't leave out the part about the night you two made love—because Aiden was with some other girl in his room."

"Is this true, Giovanni?" Aiden asked. "Is Jayla really my daughter?"

Giovanni nodded his head.

"Why didn't you tell me?" Aiden demanded.

"You see, Aiden, Giovanni was going to tell you, but he read a note in Vegas," Arturo said. "And shall I say—it fucked him up."

"Arturo, what did you do?" Aiden asked.

"Well, all I did was let Giovanni know that you fucked his beautiful wife in Tahiti," Arturo replied. "You're welcome, Giovanni—you had to find out."

"Vanni, when I say Aiden fucked your wife good, I mean Aiden fucked her good," Arturo laughed.

"Shut up, Arturo," Aiden replied. "You had no right."

"Giovanni, we didn't mean for it to happen," Aiden told him. "Guess my feelings for Katiana never stopped. But I am sorry you had to find out this way."

"Giovanni, get mad," Arturo taunted. "You just found out your brother has been banging your wife. You can't even get mad with your brother after you heard he fucked the shit out of your beautiful wife? And that she's still hiding a secret from you."

"Tell him, Aiden," Arturo pressed. "Tell Vanni the news—or shall I?"

"Shut up, Arturo. Just shut up," Aiden said, getting pissed.

"Vanni, what is Arturo talking about now? Just tell me."

"Katiana is pregnant again," Giovanni said. "By you."

"Ding, ding," Arturo replied.

"Are you sure?" Aiden asked, still in shock.

"Katiana left you a note in the hotel in Vegas saying she was late and that she was going to find out for sure," Giovanni said. Aiden grabbed his mouth.

"Every time we made love, I often wondered if she was making love to me or thinking about you," Giovanni admitted. "I know she was imagining fucking you, Aiden."

"And yes, years ago, when I slept with Katiana that night after you broke her heart... I wanted to hurt you. I married Katiana to hurt you. And what better way than to marry the one woman you truly love?"

"Watch out, Aiden!" Giovanni yelled.

Then came the sound of a gunshot.

"Oh my God, oh my God, please no!" I screamed.

"I can't lose you too," I cried. "We just lost Alex a few weeks ago."

The Story is Far from Over...

Jayla thought she had finally found stability within her new life. But the deeper she dived into her family's world, the more danger seemed to follow. Secrets are starting to unravel, betrayals cut deeper than knives, and, clearly, there are thin lines between love and survival. With Arturo looming in the shadows and the enemy's intentions growing bolder? Jayla must decide how far she's willing to go to protect the people she loves at all costs. As Part Two closes, one thing is certain: Jayla's journey is far from over. The next part of Jayla's story is just beginning.

www.ingramcontent.com/pod-product-compliance
Lightning Source LLC
Chambersburg PA
CBHW020810020726

47495CB00008B/2659